John had come to stay. The King of the Cats needed help, to guard his two royal kittens while he was away from his kingdom, and so of course he turned to his old companions John and Rosemary.

'Once every seven years,' said Carbonel, 'I and my royal brothers are summoned to the presence of The Great Cat. Every city in the world where there are cats has a king to rule over them, just as I rule over Fallowhithe. But whatever the colour, whatever the kind, when the Summons comes we must all answer.'

Of course John and Rosemary were proud to be entrusted with the kittens – but it was a difficult job with such high-spirited youngsters, especially with Queen Grisana of Broomhurst aided by Mrs Cantrip ever on the watch to trap the kittens and invade Fallowhithe – but they hardly expected it to lead to adventures like John's becoming invisible (a hungry state, he found, as he could hardly turn up for meals when Rosemary's mother couldn't see him) or being run away with by a very dim-witted magic rocking chair, and stranded all night on top of the tallest building in Fallowhithe.

If you have read Barbara Sleigh's other Puffin books, *Carbonel* and *Carbonel and Calidor*, you will already know how much excitement and entertainment she packs into her stories. As John and Rosemary say, 'A wonderful mixture of queerness and commonsense.'

BARBARA SLEIGH

The Kingdom of Carbonel

Illustrated by
Richard Kennedy

PUFFIN BOOKS

Puffin Books, Penguin Books Ltd, Harmondsworth, Middlesex, England
Viking Penguin Inc., 40 West 23rd Street, New York, New York 10010, U.S.A.
Penguin Books Australia Ltd, Ringwood, Victoria, Australia
Penguin Books Canada Ltd, 2801 John Street, Markham, Ontario, Canada L3R 1B4
Penguin Books (N.Z.) Ltd, 182–190 Wairau Road, Auckland 10, New Zealand

—

First published in the U.S.A. by Bobbs-Merrill 1960
Published in Puffin Books 1971
Reprinted 1973, 1974, 1976, 1981, 1985

—

—

Made and printed in Great Britain
by Richard Clay (The Chaucer Press) Ltd,
Bungay, Suffolk
Set in Linotype Baskerville

Contents

CONTENTS

The Green Cave

ROSEMARY BROWN picked a stick of rhubarb from the end of the garden and, taking care not to spill the sugar in the saucer she was carrying, bent herself double and crept between the currant bushes. Then she sat down in the green cave made by the unpruned branches which met over her head. The ground was covered with coarse grass, and it made a very comfortable secret place.

She dipped the rhubarb into the saucer and bit off the sweetened end with a crunch. In spite of the sugar, it was so sour that it made her nose wrinkle, so she licked the end of her finger, pressed it in the saucer and finished the sugar that way instead. When it was all gone, she lay flat on her back with her hands under her head and stared up at the summer sky which showed through the shifting chinks between the leaves.

There was half an hour before she would need to get ready to meet her friend John at the station, and the whole summer holiday lay ahead. It was nearly a year since she had seen him, but what a full year it had been! First of all there had been moving. Life was very pleasant now that she and her mother lived in the top flat at 101 Cranshaw Road, instead of in uncomfortable furnished rooms. Then there had been the fun of playing in the big, pleasantly neglected garden. Lessons, too, had gone so much better. She had worked very hard and, as a result, had won a scholarship and next term was going to the high school. Being between two schools gave her a pleasantly suspended feeling, like treading water.

Rosemary gently prodded a ladybird which had been walking over the gingham mountain of her chest. She wanted it to climb on to her finger.

'I hope it will be as much fun playing with John this holiday as it was last summer,' she said aloud to the little creature. After being headed off twice, it had obligingly clambered on to her fingernail.

'We had some glorious games,' she went on thoughtfully. 'Of course we had the garden at Tussocks to play in then.' Tussocks was the grand home of John's aunt who lived outside the town. 'But it's a funny thing, Ladybird, I can't remember what it was that was such fun when John came to play with me! It was something to do with a black cat. He was called Carbonel. And then there was an old woman whose name was Mrs Cantrip. I think,' she added slowly, 'she was a witch, and there was magic. Or did I dream that part?'

Rosemary frowned. She had a vague idea that magic and high school girls did not go together, so she shook her head in a puzzled way. 'I'm sure there was something else.'

The ladybird was now plodding laboriously up the slope of her finger. When it reached the back of her hand, it sat quite still for a moment in one of the little dapples of sunlight that filtered through the leaves, then, without any warning, spread its spotted wings and flew away.

'Of course! Flying!' said Rosemary, sitting up suddenly. 'That's what we did, and on a broomstick! Now I wonder if — '

But she never said what she wondered, for sitting at her feet, quite motionless, with his eyes closed as though he was waiting for something, was the most magnificent black cat she had ever seen. The golden flecks of sunshine gleamed on his glossy coat and the magnificent span of his whiskers. He opened his great yellow eyes as Rosemary sat up, but he did not move.

'Why,' said Rosemary, 'I was just that minute thinking of a black cat I knew once . . . or I think I did . . .

or perhaps I dreamed about ...' She tailed off lamely. The feeling that the creature had been sitting there for some time without her knowledge, combined with his unwinking golden stare, made her feel a little uncomfortable.

'Anyway,' she went on, 'you are almost as beautiful as the cat in my dream, and he was a royal cat, so you need not be offended,' she added hurriedly, almost to herself.

The animal had lifted its head in a disdainful way.

'May I stroke you?' she asked a little shyly, putting out her hand. But before she could touch him she heard her mother calling from the house.

'Rosie! Time to get ready, dear!'

Rosemary turned to the sound of her mother's voice. When she looked back again, the black cat had disappeared.

'Rosie!' called her mother faintly, but more urgently this time.

Rosemary crawled out on hands and knees, but she did not answer her mother until she reached the lawn, because she wanted to keep the Green Cave a secret.

'Coming, Mummy!' she called.

She looked back as she reached the house, and she was just in time to see a black cat leap up on to the garden wall, trot along the top and disappear behind the tool shed.

John's train was late. When it came in at last and hissed itself to a standstill, the doors burst open and people poured out in every direction. Rosemary and her mother looked anxiously up and down the busy platform, but they could not see him.

'That looks like John over there,' said Rosemary, 'but it couldn't be — he's too tall!'

But the boy came up to them, grinned and said, 'How are you, Mrs Brown? Hello, Rosie!'

He refused any help with his suitcase and walked to the gate with Mrs Brown. The two of them talked together about the journey, about John's father and mother and about how hot it was. Rosemary followed, carrying John's raincoat. Studying his back as she walked behind, she realized that she had to look up to the tuft of hair that still stood up at the back of his head. Last summer it had been level with the top of her own fair hair. He was talking to her mother in a rather grown-up way. Rosemary's heart sank.

'Well, at least his hair *does* still stick up,' she thought to herself. 'That's something, I suppose. He's come for three whole weeks, and if he's gone all grown-up since last year, whatever shall we do all the time?'

They had tea as soon as they reached home. It was a special tea, with water cress, strawberry jam and brandy snaps which Rosemary had made herself. A lot of them had broken, but she had thought it did not matter, because she and John could eat the bits afterwards in the Green Cave. Now, she did not feel sure that John was the sort of person who would enjoy the Green Cave at all.

It was a quiet meal, with Mrs Brown making most of the conversation. Afterwards, John politely offered to help wash up.

'Not when you have only just arrived, dear,' said Mrs Brown. 'But you can help Rosie clear away, then. I expect you would like to run and play in the garden. I'll see to the tea things.' She watched a little anxiously while they both stood with loaded trays, each standing back politely to let the other through the door.

When they had stacked the plates, they ran down the four flights of stairs into the garden.

'It really belongs to all the flats. The garden, I mean,' explained Rosemary. 'But the grownups hardly use it. There are no other children, so the garden is practically mine. Would you like to see my flower bed?'

They walked sedately down the path, while Rosemary tried to think of something to say.

'Did you have a good term – at school, I mean?'

'Not bad,' said John.

'Oh good!' said Rosemary. 'I'm going to the high school next term. I expect I shall have a ponytail.'

'Sally's got one. You remember, my elder sister? It was perfectly sickening. One minute she was decent – sandals and plaits, like you, and the next she wore a ponytail and high-heeled shoes, and wouldn't play anything sensible.'

Rosemary only half listened; the other half was thinking: This just can't be the same John I played with last summer who had all those glorious adventures with me. Perhaps this proves that I did dream the magic part, and the flying, and the black cat that talked.

'Goodness!' she said aloud, 'talking of black cats, there he is again!'

'I wasn't talking about black cats,' said John.

'That's the second time today,' said Rosemary excitedly. 'Look on the garden wall!'

John looked. Then he said in a matter-of-fact voice, 'I expect it's Carbonel.'

'John!' said Rosemary, and she turned to look at

him, beaming from ear to ear. 'Then it did happen! You remember the magic, and the flying and everything?'

'Of course it happened!' said John in astonishment. 'Good old Carbonel! Come on, Rosie, let's see if we can catch him!'

They ran to the garden wall and looked along it both ways, but there was no sign of the cat. John stood on the rusty old garden roller and tried to look along the top, but the roller moved when he stood on tiptoe, and he fell off on to a rubbish heap. When he sat up with leaves in his hair, Rosemary began to giggle, and presently John joined her. The invisible wall of shyness between them melted as though it had never been.

'Come on, come and see my Green Cave!' said Rosemary, as she pulled John to his feet.

They crawled in on hands and knees.

'What a glorious place!' said John, as he tucked his feet under him. There was not much room for two.

'Let's make this our headquarters!'

It was going to be all right after all, thought Rosemary, and she ferreted happily under a pile of leaves and brought out the broken brandy snaps in a biscuit tin. They sat and munched happily together.

'I'm not really going to have a ponytail,' said Rosemary suddenly.

'You are an owl, Rosie!' said John, and tweaked one of her plaits in a friendly way. 'Come on, let's go and play something!'

2

Carbonel Again

MRS BROWN was a widow. She added to her small pension by dressmaking. The house in Cranshaw Road belonged to Mr Featherstone, who ran a travelling Repertory Company called the Netherley Players. Instead of paying rent for the flat, Rosemary's mother looked after the costumes of the Company. These were kept in the old stables of the house.

After breakfast next morning, Mrs Brown said, 'Rosie, dear, I've got to get on with those Roman togas in the costume room this morning – simply miles of machining, so will you and John do some shopping for me?'

They fetched a basket. With the shopping list on the outside of an old envelope and a pound note inside, they ran downstairs.

'Good Heavens!' said John, as they closed the front door behind them. 'There he is again!'

Sure enough, on top of one of the stone balls that stood on each gatepost, sat Carbonel. As soon as John and Rosemary reached the gate, he dropped silently down beside them.

'Good morning!' said Rosemary politely. 'We're going shopping, but we shan't be long.'

'It's a funny thing,' said John, 'but he makes me feel I ought to bow to him. Hallo! He's following.'

Carbonel was trotting quietly at their heels. He went with them to the bakers, and the fishmonger's,

and the grocer's and the little shop that sold news-
papers and sweets and ices.

Once, they tried to see if they could shake him off
by running quickly round a corner and diving down
a little alley. But when they came out of the alleyway,
after waiting for several minutes, the black cat was
sitting at the entrance, quietly washing his paws,
which made them feel rather silly. The only difference
was that from that moment on he walked beside
instead of behind them, as though he intended that
they should not escape.

On the way home, they sat down on a seat by the
side of a quiet road to eat the ice-creams they had
bought at the little shop. They licked in silence, and
Carbonel sat at their feet and stared and stared at
them.

'He's beginning to make me feel uncomfortable,'
said John.

'Do you think he's hungry?' suggested Rosemary.

'Doesn't . . . look . . . like it. Fat . . . as butter,' replied
John in the jerky way of someone whose tongue is
occupied with capturing escaping ice cream.

'Now you've offended him!' said Rosemary re-
proachfully. Carbonel had turned his back on John
and was gazing up at Rosemary. '*Are* you hungry,
Carbonel?'

She held out the packet of fish. It was one of those
very fishy parcels. Carbonel's nose quivered slightly
at the enticing smell, but he closed his eyes resolutely
and opened his mouth in a disdainful yawn.

'Well, it's clearly not that,' said John. 'Listen, Carbonel –' he went on. But the animal continued to
sit with his back turned, as though John did not
exist.

'I expect you'd better apologize, John,' said Rosemary.

John muttered something under his breath and then thought better of it.

'I'm sorry, Carbonel, honestly I am. I forgot how touchy you are. But I do wish to goodness we knew what was the matter!'

'Do you want to tell us something?' said Rosemary. Carbonel turned and, putting his front paws on Rosemary's knee, licked the back of her hand with a warm, rasping tongue.

'But how can you tell us?' asked John.

Greatly daring, Rosemary stooped down and gathered the black cat into her arms, because she felt he needed comforting. He was so heavy that it was quite an effort. She put him on her knee. He no longer fitted into the hollow of her lap, and she had to hold him with both arms or he would have overflowed on to the wooden seat.

'We'd do anything we could to help you, Carbonel. Wouldn't we, John?'

John nodded. 'But how can we tell what is the matter if you can't talk to us? What can we do?'

'Why don't we consult Mrs Cantrip?' suggested John. 'I know she is supposed to have retired from being a witch, but perhaps we could persuade her to tell us if there is anything we could do. Hi! Carbonel!' he protested.

At the mention of Mrs Cantrip, Carbonel stood up on Rosemary's knee and, with a deep, bass purr, thrust the top of his sleek head against her chin again and again. Then he jumped on to John's lap, upsetting the shopping basket so that fish, biscuits, bacon and sugar went rolling on to the ground. They stuffed them back into the basket and set off home, Carbonel with tail erect, trotting before them.

'The last time I saw Mrs Cantrip she was washing-up at the Copper Kettle tea rooms,' said Rosemary. 'I don't know if she is still there.'

'Let's go and see,' said John.

*   *   *

They set out for the Copper Kettle early after lunch. Carbonel was waiting for them on the gatepost. They explained where they were going, but, instead of coming with them, the black cat showed complete indifference. He sat down in the middle of the pavement and began to wash his tail. John and Rosemary walked past, but Carbonel caught up with them and calmly placed himself in front of them again. This time he transferred his attention to his left hind leg.

'Well,' said John, 'you'd better hurry if you want us to go and find Mrs Cantrip, Carbonel, because I'm not going without you and that's final.'

Carbonel gave him a withering glance, then trotted ahead, keeping pointedly to Rosemary's side of the pavement. Having decided to go with them, he set off at such a speed that they could barely keep up, and when they finally reached the Copper Kettle, which was some distance away, they were hot and footsore.

Miss Maggie and her sister Florrie, who owned the teashop, were old friends. They welcomed the two children with cries of pleasure. Carbonel waited outside.

'Why, if it isn't John! And how you've grown!' said Miss Maggie with upraised hands. As everyone of a still-growing age knows, there is no answer to this, so John merely grinned sheepishly.

17

'Now, come into the kitchen, dears. We're just putting away the lunch things. Choose whatever you'd like to eat. How about some nice fruit salad?'

John winked at Rosie as they followed Miss Maggie. Fruit salad was always welcome, and Mrs Cantrip would probably be found in the kitchen.

But, standing at the sink in a cloud of steam, was not Mrs Cantrip, but a square, vigorous young woman who was accompanying her saucepan cleaning by singing a rather doleful hymn tune. This was a thing that Mrs Cantrip would certainly not have done.

'To tell the truth, dear,' said Miss Maggie in reply to Rosemary's inquiries, 'I was quite glad when the funny old thing left of her own accord. Want some more cream on your fruit, dear?'

Rosemary nodded. She finished the last of the pineapple, which she did not really like, and prepared to enjoy the pears and peaches.

'I'm always saying to Florrie,' went on Miss Maggie. 'Florrie, I say, if there's one thing I hate it's unpleasantness! And really she was so very queer that I never knew quite how she'd take it if I told her to leave.'

'So it wasn't you who fired her?' asked John.

'Would you believe it? She went off one evening in the middle of the week? Put her shoes and apron in the cupboard under the sink, just as usual, and never turned up again, and with half a week's wages to come!'

'We'd send it on to her if we knew the address,' said Miss Florrie, who had come in while her sister was talking. 'But she never would tell us where she lived.'

'Not that she did her work badly, mind you,' continued Miss Maggie. 'I will say that. Now it's no good for you to sniff like that, Doris,' she said to the new girl. 'Fair's fair. But her washing-up water! I do like it clean! She always seemed to get hers not exactly dirty but coloured, somehow – bright red or yellow or green. I can't imagine how she did it.'

John and Rosemary looked at one another.

'And when I spoke to her about it once,' went on Miss Maggie, 'she said something about clean water being so dull. Did you ever hear of such a thing?'

Conversation became general after this. Presently Rosemary said, 'If you like, John and I could take Mrs Cantrip's money to her, and her shoes. She used to keep a little shop in Fairfax Market.'

'Well, that would be kind of you, dears!' said Miss Maggie.

She rummaged in the cupboard under the sink and brought out an enormous pair of buckled shoes of a very expensive make, but very down at the heel. The apron had a vivid pattern of flowers and tropical fruit. As Miss Maggie shook it out, a little screw of paper fell from the pocket on to the floor. By the time Rosemary had picked it up, the shoes and the apron had already been made into a neat roll, so she put the paper in her own pocket. As soon as they could, John and Rosemary said good-bye.

Carbonel paused in his restless pacing as soon as he saw them.

'Well, if we can find her in her own house, it will really be much better than trying to talk to her at the Copper Kettle with Miss Maggie buzzing round,' John said, when they had explained the situation.

But Carbonel did not wait for him to finish. He bounded off in the direction of Fairfax Market so quickly that the children did not attempt to keep up with him.

'Well!' said Rosemary.

'If he isn't at Mrs Cantrip's house when we get there, I vote we just go away and do nothing more about it,' said John.

'I almost hope he won't be!' said Rosemary.

But he was. When they reached the little shop that had been Mrs Cantrip's last year, the black cat was sitting beside the door with what John called his 'waiting expression'.

'Supposing Mrs Cantrip doesn't live here any more,' said Rosemary hopefully.

'She lives here all right!' said John. 'Look at the curtains!'

There was no longer any trace of a shop. The grimy window was hung with two odd lengths of lace, looped up in an attempt at elegance. One was tied with a boot-lace, and the other with a piece of purple ribbon that looked as though it had come off a chocolate box.

'They aren't very clean,' said Rosemary.

Someone had started to paint the battered front door scarlet, but had lost interest halfway down.

'I say! Look at that notice!' said John.

Propped against the window was a card which said, in wobbly capital letters,

APARTMENTS

H. and C. in all rooms.

R.S.V.P.

As they looked at it in silence, a bony hand appeared between the dusty curtains and took away the card. John squared his shoulders. 'She's at home all right. Here goes!' he said, and he knocked loudly on the door.

In reply to his second knock, the door opened a
crack and a voice that was unmistakably Mrs Cantrip's
said, 'Apartments is let! Go away!' And the door was
firmly slammed in their faces.

When John knocked again, there was no answer, so
he pushed open the flap of the letter box and called
through, 'Do let us in, Mrs Cantrip, we've got something for you!' But he backed away suddenly when
he saw a pair of piercing eyes staring at him from the
other side of the letterbox.

Rosemary, who had been trying to see, too, nearly
fell over when the door was suddenly flung open.

'Got something for me, have you?' said Mrs Cantrip. 'That's different, that is! Come inside!'

She stood blinking and bobbing at the open door
while the children waited uncertainly on the step. A
furry pressure on the back of the knees from Carbonel,
which might have been affection, or even a plain
shove, sent John stumbling down the step into the
house, which was below the level of the road. Of
course Rosemary followed.

3

Prism Powder

MRS CANTRIP led the way into an inner room. There was very little furniture, but it was tidy, and on the rickety table was a jam jar which held a bunch of nettles and dandelions. The familiar golden flower faces made Rosemary feel a little braver.

The old woman sat down in a rocking chair by the smouldering fire.

'Well,' she said eagerly, 'hand it over!'

'It's from Miss Maggie at The Copper Kettle,' said Rosemary. 'She asked us to give you the shoes and the apron you left behind, and the money she owes you.'

As she spoke she put them on the table. Mrs Cantrip hardly bothered to look.

'Do you mean to say that's all?' she snorted. 'Coming into my house under false pretences, I call it. I could have fetched them for myself any day.' She started to rock herself violently in the rocking chair, pushing herself off with her big feet.

'Miss Maggie wondered why you didn't,' said Rosemary.

'Why did you leave?' asked John.

'Because the sight of her stirring away at her pots and saucepans made my fingers itch! Hours she spent over her magic books and her mixtures, and never so much as a puff of coloured smoke to show for it! Let alone turning anyone into anything satisfactory, like a blowfly or a spider!'

'But of course she didn't' said Rosemary indignantly. 'She wasn't trying to. That isn't how you run a teashop! She was making nice things to eat out of cookery books, not magic!'

Mrs Cantrip snorted again.

'Incompetent I call it. And anyway, I'm letting apartments instead. H. and C. in all rooms.' She nodded with satisfaction. 'R.S.V.P.'

'Have you really got hot and cold water?' asked John.

'Who said anything about water?'

'Well, that's what it usually means,' said Rosemary.

'Not when I use it, it doesn't,' snapped Mrs Cantrip rocking with renewed vigour. 'It means air. Cold when the window is open, hot when it's shut – if you build up a good fire. It's up to you. The postman taught me a tidy bit of magic to get a lodger.'

'The postman?' said Rosemary in surprise.

'That's what I said! He brought me an invitation to a ball once, by mistake. But a bit of cardboard always comes in handy, so I kept it.'

'But you shouldn't –' began Rosemary.

Mrs Cantrip ignored her. 'At the bottom of the card it said R.S.V.P. I asked the postman what it meant, and he said it was foreign for 'You've got to answer.' A magic rune, you see. That's what I call practical. So I put R.S.V.P. on my card in the window, and it worked. In half an hour I got a lodger and then, because I didn't undo the R.S.V.P. straight away, you two came along.'

'But we don't –' began John.

'That's a good thing, because you can't. There's no room. Apartments I said, and I'm not having togetherments, not with nobody.'

Rosemary looked hopelessly at John. They seemed no nearer to the real object of their visit.

'Mrs Cantrip,' interrupted John firmly. 'We want to ask you something. It's about Carbonel!'

Mrs Cantrip ceased speaking in mid-sentence and stopped rocking the chair. For a minute, there was complete silence in the dark little kitchen.

'That animal again!' said Mrs Cantrip, in a hoarse whisper. 'Who are you?'

'We are John and Rosemary. Don't you remember? When you retired from being a witch last summer, you sold me your old broom and your cat, Carbonel, and John and I set him free from your spell to be King of the Cats again. We want you to help us.'

The knuckles of Mrs Cantrip's bony hands showed white where she held the arms of the rocking chair, and her small eyes bored into them like needles.

'Oh, ah! I remember the pair of you now. Interfering busybodying children. What do you want?'

'Carbonel is in trouble,' said Rosemary. 'At least I'm pretty sure he is, and he can't make us understand. Won't you help us?'

'Why should I help Carbonel?' said the old woman, in a voice as cold as steel. 'Did he ever help me? Not him. He hampered me at every turn! Besides,' she added sulkily, 'I've gone out of business, you know that. Broom, books, cauldron – all gone, and everything as dull as puddle water.'

'What about the washing-up water at The Copper Kettle? How did you make it turn red and green?' said John accusingly.

Mrs Cantrip's eyes wavered.

'That wasn't what you'd call magic. Not real magic,' she muttered. 'Just using up odds and ends of spells I'd got left over. You wouldn't have me be wasteful, now would you?' she said virtuously. 'I couldn't throw

them away. Some dear little child might have picked
them up, and then what would have happened to him?'
She grinned wickedly. 'It's nearly all gone. I just use
a pinch here and a spoonful there, to liven things up
a bit. And that reminds me, where's that apron?'

She pounced on the bundle that was lying on the
table, shook out the apron, and felt feverishly in the
pocket.

'It's gone! It isn't here! My last little bit of Prism
Powder! What have you done with it?'

Rosemary felt hurriedly in her own pocket. The
little ball of paper she had picked up from the floor of
the Copper Kettle was still there.

'If I give you back your Prism Powder, will you tell
us what we can do to understand Carbonel when he
talks to us?'

There was a pause.

'All right, I'll tell you! I'll tell you and willing!'
said Mrs Cantrip, eagerly holding out her hand.

'Wait a minute,' said John. 'You shall have it when
you have told us what to do and not before!'

Mrs Cantrip pursed her mouth to the size of a key-
hole and rubbed the side of her great nose with a bony
finger.

'I can't do it myself, not now. That would never
do. I know. I'll give you a prescription and you must
have it made up by a druggist.'

'By a druggist!' said John.

Mrs Cantrip ignored him. She was ferreting around
in the drawer of the table, among bits of string and
candle ends. Presently she fished out a crumpled bit
of paper, and fetching a bottle of ink and a rather
moth-eaten quill pen from the mantelpiece, sat down
at the table. For a minute she sucked the end of her

pen, then she chuckled, smoothed out the paper, and began writing with great speed. When she had finished, she folded the paper and handed it to Rosemary.

Both children were craning over to see what she was writing, and they were quite unprepared for the pounce that the old woman made on the ball of paper that Rosemary had brought out of her pocket. They unfolded the note she had given them and stared at it.

'But it isn't writing! It looks like nonsense!' said Rosemary.

Mrs Cantrip took no notice. She was undoing the paper. Inside was about a saltspoonful of what looked like tiny grains of multi-coloured candy.

'Take it to Hedgem and Fudge to have it made up. Now go away. I'm busy.'

As she spoke she dropped a single grain of the powder into the ink bottle. There was a slight hiss, and the muddy-looking ink turned a brilliant scarlet. She dropped another grain into the bottle and the ink changed to pure yellow. Her grim face softened.

'Good Heavens!' said John with interest.

'Go away,' said Mrs Cantrip fiercely, shielding the bottle with her hands.

There seemed nothing else to do, so they went.

4

Hedgem and Fudge

JOHN and Rosemary closed the front door behind them and stood blinking in the sunlight. It was like coming out of a cave. Carbonel stopped his restless pacing and ran to them with an anxious little 'Prrt!'

'She's given us a prescription, and we've got to get it made up at a drugstore called Hedgem and Fudge. It looks like nothing but a lot of squiggles to me,' said John.

'But so do the prescriptions that doctors write,' said Rosemary. 'What's the matter, Carbonel?'

'I think he wants to read it,' said John.

Rosemary bent down and laid the piece of paper on the sidewalk. Carbonel held it down with one paw and stared at it with unblinking yellow eyes. They waited anxiously while he examined it. First he sniffed it with delicately twitching whiskers. Then he sneezed violently. Finally, he removed his paw and shook it with distaste. But he purred loudly, and gave each of the children an approving lick on a bare leg, and set off at a gallop in the direction of the High Street, looking back from time to time to see that they were following.

'It's all so strange,' said John breathlessly, as they hurried after him. 'Such a mixture of queerness and commonsense!'

'I know,' said Rosemary. 'And whoever could be going as a boarder to Mrs Cantrip? Oh, goodness! I believe Hedgem and Fudge is that big chemist near the Cathedral!'

'We shall look pretty silly if we hand over a page of gibberish and say "I want this made up, please!"' said John gloomily.

But no one can be gloomy for long if he is running, so Rosemary and John stopped talking because they needed all their breath to keep up with Carbonel. Once, in the High Street full of afternoon shoppers, they thought they had lost him, and several times they bumped into people and had to stop and apologize. When Carbonel reached the top of the High Street where the road widens in front of the Cathedral, he waited for them to catch up.

'There it is!' said Rosemary. 'That's the shop on the other side of the road!'

It was a large, old-fashioned building. Above the cars that honked and hurried, they could see the name in gold letters, as well as two great glass bottles full of glowing red and green liquid that have been the sign of a dispenser of medicine since the days when few people could read.

There was a screeching of brakes as Carbonel stepped without warning on to the pedestrian crossing and with great dignity, tail erect, swept across the road. The drivers who were not angry grinned.

Very red about the ears, John and Rosemary crossed the road behind him.

Although the building was clearly an old one, the shop had been brought up to date inside. Behind the counter, there were rows of little mahogany drawers with cut-glass handles which sparkled in the strip lighting. There were steel chairs to sit on, and a counter, which displayed face powder and lipsticks and shampoos, with a yellow-haired young lady behind it. A smaller counter displayed castor oil, cough medicines and headache pills, with a pink young man behind it. On this counter was a notice which said, PRESCRIPTIONS, so Rosemary handed the piece of paper to the young man.

He took it and glanced casually at the writing. Then suddenly his eyebrows shot up and his neck seemed to lengthen as he peered at the paper.

'Wait for it!' said John under his breath to Rosemary.

But far from being angry, the young man said, 'Excuse me one minute!' and went to consult an older man who was busy in a glass-partitioned dispensary at the back of the shop. They whispered together for a while, and then the older man came over to the counter. First he read the prescription again through his spectacles, then he peered over them at John and Rosemary.

'This is most unusual,' he said. 'I have never been asked for it before. However, it is not for me to question a prescription.'

He turned to the young man. 'You'd better fetch the steps from the back, Mr Flackett.'

'What is he going to do?' Rosemary asked John anxiously.

'Ask me another! I only hope Mrs Cantrip hasn't double-crossed us!' said John.

The young man put the steps against the mahogany partition that divided the window from the shop, and mounted them gingerly, while the older man held them steady. Then he put both arms round the huge glass bottle of red liquid that they had seen from the other side of the road, and breathing heavily with the effort, tottered dangerously down the steps with it into the dispensary.

John and Rosemary stood and listened to the fair-haired young lady serving a customer until the young man returned with a small medicine bottle full of red liquid. There was a pink mark down the front of his white jacket which he was rubbing with his handkerchief.

'Such an awkward thing to pour from,' he said to Rosemary, who noticed that his fingers were stained with the liquid. He wrapped up the bottle in white paper which he fastened at each end with a little blob of sealing wax.

'Excuse me while I look it up in the price list,' he said, flicking over the leaves of a catalogue. He licked his pink-stained thumb several times the better to turn the pages.

Now this is a horrible habit as everyone knows, but what followed may have cured him forever. He turned to speak to John and Rosemary, and suddenly started. His mouth fell open and all the pink ebbed from his face, leaving it a curious greenish white.

'Are you all right?' asked Rosemary sympathetically.

The young man swallowed hard.

'It's a funny thing,' he said faintly, 'but I distinctly thought I heard that black cat beside you speak! There is a black cat, isn't there?' he asked anxiously.

John and Rosemary looked down. There was indeed. It was Carbonel. Tired of waiting outside, he had followed an old lady through the swinging door into the shop. The children looked at each other.

'What did you think he said?' John asked tactfully.

The now pale young man swallowed hard again.

'He said, in a cross voice, "Royalty, and left outside to wait like an old umbrella!" It doesn't even make sense,' said the young man unhappily.

'That sounds like Carbonel all right!' said John to Rosemary. The black cat stood between them, his ears slightly flattened and his tail twitching. The young man stared fascinated at the cat, and his colour began to come back, but he started violently once more.

'He's done it again!' he said miserably. 'He says – the cat I mean – to tell you not to take all day about it. Couldn't you hear him, too?' he pleaded.

'No!' said John and Rosemary. 'We couldn't, truthfully.'

'But a cat talking! Whatever does it mean?' asked the young man anxiously.

'I expect it means that you've eaten something that has disagreed with you,' said Rosemary truthfully.

'I should take some Peterson's Pink Pills,' said John. They were the first thing that caught his eye. 'And go to bed early. Good afternoon! Come on, Rosie!'

He picked up the bottle from the counter and hurried Rosemary from the shop, Carbonel trotting at their heels.

'But the poor young man! Shouldn't we try to do something for him?' Rosemary said.

'My good girl, what can we do?' said John. 'I expect it will wear off in time, and if Carbonel had gone on talking in there, the poor man might have gone completely off his rocker. I suggest we don't open this bottle till we get back to the Green Cave. We don't want any more complications. Come on, let's run!'

5

The Red Mixture

IT was long past teatime when John and Rosemary reached home. Mrs Brown was not there. In her place was a plate with some crumbs on it, and a note propped against the sugar basin which said, COULDN'T WAIT. WON'T HANG. GET YOUR OWN.

Rosemary explained that this meant her mother had gone back to the sewing-room because the dress she was making would not fall in the folds she wanted, and that they were to see about tea for themselves.

'I'm terribly hungry,' said John. 'Let's take it with us to the Green Cave.'

They put a plate of buns and two pieces of cake on a tray. Rosemary added cups of tea, and a saucer of milk for Carbonel; then they carried it into the garden.

The black cat was waiting for them on the path by the currant bushes. As soon as he saw them, he disappeared among the leaves, and when John and Rosemary wriggled after him, with some difficulty because of the tea tray, they found him in the Green Cave sitting serenely on the rusty biscuit tin which had held the brandy snaps. Looking up at him from the kneeling position that was necessary in the cramped space between the bushes, they were a little awed by his quiet dignity. He was looking fixedly at the bottle which they had put on the tray.

'Come on! Let's see what the directions say,' said

John, as he tore off the wrapping paper. 'It has an ordinary chemist's label. "The Mixture,"' he read. ' "Half a teaspoon to be taken after meals as required." Well, I'm always requiring meals. I'm requiring my tea like billy-oh!'

'I don't think it means "meals as required",' said Rosemary, 'but "the mixture as required – after meals".'

'Oh,' said John. 'Well, let's hurry up and have our tea now. I'm starving!'

They each took a currant bun which they polished off with not much politeness but with great speed. Carbonel ignored the saucer of milk which Rosemary had poured for him. He sat staring expectantly at the children with wide, golden eyes.

'We'd better eat the cake, too, to make it a meal,' said John. 'One bun is just a snack.'

They finished the cake and drank the tea. What had not slopped in the saucers was cold and rather nasty, but Rosemary swallowed every drop of hers very slowly, because she found herself wanting to put off the moment of drinking the strange, red mixture. John was clearly feeling the same way.

'Look here,' he said. 'There can't be anything to be afraid of. The chemist's assistant could hear Carbonel talking, when he licked his thumb with the red liquid on it, so we know it does what we want it to do. Let's drink at exactly the same minute, then whatever it is will happen to us both at the same time.'

Rosemary nodded, Carbonel came down from the tin, and purring encouragement, rubbed his head against her shoulder. They took their teaspoons and half filled them with the liquid, which fell sluggishly from the bottle. It had a strange, heady smell, rather like crushed chrysanthemum leaves. They knelt together with spoons raised.

'I'll say "One, two, three, go!"' said John.

Rosemary nodded again. She became aware that, except for John's voice, it was very still in the Green Cave. Even the canopy of leaves above them had ceased its restless stirring. The only moving things were two fat caterpillars with tufted backs, making their way slowly along a twig on a level with Rosemary's nose. She stared at them unheedingly while John said, 'One! Two! Three! Go!'

Rosemary took a deep breath, swallowed the spoonful quickly, and shut her eyes.

Behind the red darkness of her tightly closed lids, she felt the liquid fizzing slightly on her tongue. It tasted sharp, but not unpleasant, and glowed comfortingly as it slipped down her throat. There was a tickling in her nose and a tight, uncomfortable feeling in her ears. She felt an enormous sneeze welling up inside her, the father and mother of all sneezes. She tried to fight it down, but it was no good. Suddenly she shattered the silence with three violent sneezes, each one echoed closely by another from John. The two children looked at each other with startled eyes.

The silence was gone. They were surrounded by what at first sounded like a humming noise. Then the hum seemed to break up into innumerable little voices, some high and shrill, some soft and purring, some abrupt as the plucking of a violin string. Rosemary was startled to distinguish a small, singsong voice quite close to her ear saying over and over again, 'Up we go! Up we go!'

She looked around, and saw with astonishment that it was the second of the two caterpillars.

'Where are you going?' she asked.

The second caterpillar halted for a moment, waved its front half about uncertainly, and then hurried after its companion.

'Don't look round now,' it said breathlessly, 'but I think we're being spoken to – by a human! What a mercy the great blundering things can't hear us talking!'

'But I *can* hear you talking!' said Rosemary, a little nettled at being called 'blundering'.

Both the caterpillars turned around in astonishment, lost their balance and fell off the twig onto the grass below in two tightly rolled coils from which they refused to budge.

'Rosie!' said John. 'There's a super beetle here, all green and blue, and he says –'

'John and Rosemary, will you kindly pay attention!'

They turned to where Carbonel sat enthroned on the biscuit tin, the end of his tail twitching in irritation.

'That is, of course, unless you find the conversation of beetles and caterpillars more worth while than mine!'

'Carbonel! How glorious!' said Rosemary happily. 'We can hear you talking, too!'

'Which is not much use unless you're prepared to listen. After all the trouble I've taken with you!'

'The trouble *you've* taken with *us*!' said John.

But Carbonel swept on. 'I thought I should never get you to understand what I wanted, and when at last you did realize you had to find Mrs Cantrip, and I tried to stop you from wasting your time by going off to the Copper Kettle, would you take any notice? Oh, dear me, no!'

'Don't let's waste time now by being cross!' said Rosemary. 'We did the best we could, and we never expected to be able to hear beetles and caterpillars talking as well as you. It is rather exciting, you know!'

She put out her hand, and laid it gently over the angry, twitching end of Carbonel's tail. For a moment she could feel it stirring beneath her palm. Then, gradually, the furry movement slowed down and ceased altogether.

'Oh, come off it, Carbonel!' said John affectionately.

The black cat took him at his word and stepped down from the box.

'Very well,' he said. 'I have no doubt you did do your best, and I am grateful. And I must say, you were very quick witted to bargain with *her* for the prescription. Now, pay attention, both of you, because I don't have much time. I have not gone to all this trouble for the pleasure of a mere chat, though I won't deny I am pleased to see you both again. Very pleased. I need your help.'

'Of course we'll help you! Won't we, John?' said Rosemary.

'Tomorrow I must go away,' Carbonel said.

'Go away!' said Rosemary in dismay. 'Where to?'

'And when we've just found out how to talk to you!' said John.

'There you go again! Listen, and I will explain. You know that I am a royal cat, and that my people have their own laws and customs. After dark, the wall tops are our highways and the roofs our mountains and our plains. The Town Hall has been the royal seat of my ancestors for two hundred years, and there I hope my descendants will rule after me. Now that is where I need your help. My royal children —'

'Kittens! Your kittens!' said Rosemary excitedly. 'Carbonel, how lovely! How many have you got? And why didn't you tell us? We should –'

'I am trying to tell you now!' said Carbonel severely.

'But –'

'Shut up, Rosie!' said John under his breath.

'You may not know,' went on Carbonel, 'that it is our custom for each cat to select a human family to look after.'

'Don't you mean the humans choose a cat?' said John.

'Certainly not!' said Carbonel coldly. 'The humans, of course, repay a little of their debt to us with a place by the fire, a saucer of milk, little offerings of fish and meat according to their humble means.'

'But besides catching mice, what –' began John. It was Rosemary's turn to give a warning nudge.

'Our great gift to the human race is our example.'

'Example?'

'That is what I said. You fuss and flurry and rush about all day, and for what? In the midst of it all, we sit calm and unruffled, meditating on the mystery of Life and Eternity.'

'But your kittens,' said Rosemary. 'Do tell us about them! How many are there? And are they like you? Oh, I must see them.'

'There are two of them, a boy and a girl,' said Carbonel. 'They are said to be remarkably handsome – but whether they are like me you must judge for yourselves,' he added modestly.

'Then we can see them?'

'Certainly. I have chosen you to look after them while I am away.'

'Of course we'll look after them for you! We'd love

to, wouldn't we, John? I shall have to ask Mother, of course, but I'm sure she will say yes.'

'Guard them faithfully till I come back.'

'When will that be?' asked John.

'Three days? Three weeks? Three months? Who can tell?'

'But why must you go?' persisted John.

'Once every seven years I and my royal brothers are summoned to the presence of the Great Cat.'

'But who are your royal brothers?' asked Rosemary.

'You must not think that I am the only cat king,' explained Carbonel. 'Every city in the world where there are cats has a king to rule over them, just as I rule over the cats of Fallowhithe. When the Summons comes, we must all obey. There will be lean, blue-eyed cats from Siam, long-haired cats from Persia, great tawny jungle cats, and thin, big-boned cats from Egypt. Cats of every colour – black as coal, white as milk, grey as woodsmoke. Whatever the colour, whatever the kind, when the Summons comes we all must answer.'

'But who will look after your kingdom for you while you are away?' asked John.

'My beautiful Queen, my lovely Blandamour, will rule with the help of my cousin Merbeck. Blandamour is wise and good, but I cannot answer for all the queens of the neighbouring towns. Queen Grisana of Broomhurst is ambitious, and her husband is old. Do not let my kittens stray. They are a little –' There was a pause, as though Carbonel were searching for the right word. 'High spirited,' he concluded. 'Early to-morrow morning, before I go, I shall visit you again and bring my royal children with me.'

It was getting dark in the Green Cave, and the shadow that was Carbonel slipped silently down from the cooky jar and rubbed against Rosemary, and his purring filled the little space under the currant bushes like an organ. A warm tongue licked her cheek.

'Dear Carbonel!' said Rosemary, putting her arms around him for a minute. 'Of course we'll do our best to take care of your kittens, but do you think –'

She broke off. The black cat had slipped from her and melted into the other shadows.

6

The Royal Kittens

THEY did not ask that night if they might have the kittens after all. Rosemary felt that her mother was not in a 'yes-of-course-darling' mood. She was still having trouble with a dress she was making, and only looked in to tell them to take the sausages on the cracked plate for supper.

'Never mind,' said John. 'You can ask at breakfast tomorrow. Don't forget, Carbonel said he was coming early.'

But Carbonel's idea of early was rather different from theirs.

Rosemary was awakened next morning by a fly which buzzed persistently around her pillow. She brushed it away with a sleepy hand once or twice, and turned over; but the fly continued to buzz. Presently she became aware that it was not just buzzing. It was saying over and over again in a shrill, angry voice, 'For goodness' sake, wake up!'

Rosemary opened one eye sleepily, and saw the fly a few inches away on the curve of her pillow. It was jumping up and down angrily on all of its six legs.

'I am awake,' said Rosemary sleepily, and gave a cavernous yawn.

The fly made a noise that sounded like an outraged squeak, and braced itself.

'Don't do that,' it said in an agitated voice. 'I once knew a fly who was swallowed by a yawn!'

'How horrible!' said Rosemary, thinking more of

the yawner than the fly. She was wide awake now and sitting up.

'Here am I, simply come to deliver a message to oblige, and my very life is threatened! First you go flapping like a windmill, and then –'

'I'm so sorry,' said Rosemary humbly.

'And you should be,' said the fly a little more calmly. 'Many people would just have flown off without delivering the message. But not me. I'm not that kind of fly. Luckily for you, I have a weakness for royalty.'

'Royalty?' interrupted Rosemary. 'Is it from Carbonel? The message, I mean.'

The fly nodded importantly.

'I was just to tell you, "We are here." Kings talk like that, you know,' it added condescendingly.

'But where is "here"?' asked Rosemary.

'The greenhouse at the bottom of the garden. Oh! There you go again!'

Without warning, Rosemary had flung back the bed-clothes and jumped out of bed. Buzzing angrily, the fly circled round her as she dressed.

'I am sorry!' she said again, 'and of course I'm very grateful to you, but I must go and tell John at once. I think I've got some sugar you can have somewhere.'

She felt in the pocket of her school blazer and brought out a rather dusty sugar lump, which she put on the dressing table. Then, in one movement, she pushed her toes into her slippers and her arms into her dressing gown.

John and Rosemary did not waste time dressing. They crept downstairs into the shining, early morning garden. It was so early that the shadows were still long and narrow, and the dew from the grass, which needed cutting, was cold on their bare ankles.

The birds and the small daylight creatures were all awake. The faint hum that Rosemary and John had noticed after drinking the red mixture was all around them, like the hum of a busy market place, but fainter and on a higher note. If they stood still, they could distinguish the little voices of which it was made. Only the birds sang loudly and excitedly of all the things they hoped to do on such a glorious day. Rosemary wanted to stop and listen, but John pulled her on.

The greenhouse was quite small. It had not been used for some time. The lock was broken, and several of the panes were cracked. The coloured tiles patterning the floor had come loose from their moorings and rocked beneath Rosemary's and John's feet when they walked on them. The greenhouse no longer held rows of pots, full of delicate flowers. There was only one remaining climbing plant which had run riot over the walls and roof. Mrs Brown called it plumbago. It was flowering now, and great trusses of pale blue blossoms hung among the dark green leaves. John and Rosemary ran down the path and opened the door.

On the shelf which had once housed pots of geraniums and primulas and lacy ferns, before a curtain of blue flowers, sat Carbonel. Beside him was a snow-white Persian, and between them were two kittens, one coal-black with white paws and the other tortoise-shell. All four sat quite still with their tails wrapped neatly around their front paws from left to right. The children hesitated by the open door. A blue flower fell silently between the kittens, and the black one raised a paw as if to pat it.

'Calidor!' said Carbonel sternly, and the kitten instantly wrapped his tail round his paws again, as if that would keep them out of mischief.

'Good morning, Rosemary. Good morning, John.'

'Good morning,' said the children together, and John, to his surprise, found himself adding, 'Sir.'

'My dear,' said Carbonel, turning to the white cat. 'I have great pleasure in presenting my two friends, John and Rosemary.'

The white cat gazed at them with wide, faraway blue eyes and bowed her head graciously. 'My husband has often spoken of you. His friends will always be mine.'

'Thank you,' said John rather lamely.

'Present the children, my love,' said Blandamour. Carbonel bent his head in acknowledgement.

'My son, Prince Calidor, and my daughter, Princess Pergamond. Make your bows, my children.'

The two kittens stood up, and with back legs splayed

out and small tails erect, made rather wobbly bows. John bobbed his head, and Rosemary lifted the skirt of her nightdress and made a little curtsy.

'I give my children into your care,' said Carbonel. 'Protect their nine lives as if they were your own. And you, my children, repeat the royal rules each day and put them into practice.'

'Yes, Father,' said the kittens in shrill chorus.

'And obey John and Rosemary in all things.'

'Yes, Father.'

'Remember, they are in your charge and you are in theirs.'

'Yes, Father.'

'And when I come back, let me hear nothing to your discredit.'

The black kitten, whose eyes had wandered to the drifting blue flowers again, began to say 'Yes, Father,' and hastily changed it to 'No.'

Carbonel turned to Blandamour. 'My love, it is time for me to go. Come with me to the crossroads and see me on my way.'

The black cat jumped silently to the tiled floor and went out into the sunlit garden, and Blandamour followed. John and Rosemary, watching them leap to the top of the garden wall, ran to wave good-bye. Standing on the garden roller, their chins level with the top of the wall, they could see Carbonel and Blandamour growing smaller and smaller as they trotted along the wall. It skirted the end of the gardens of number one hundred, number ninety-nine and number ninety-eight. At number ninety-seven, the wall curved, and the two cats disappeared from view.

'Well, that's that!' said John, jumping down from

the roller and wiping the moss from his hands on to his pyjamas.

'Come on. Let's get back to the kittens. Aren't they gorgeous!' said Rosemary.

They ran back to the greenhouse. To their surprise, only the tortoise-shell kitten was to be seen. She was standing on her hind paws on a flower pot, peering into an old watering can.

'Where's the other one? Where's Calidor?' asked Rosemary, looking round anxiously.

'He's in here,' said Pergamond in a muffled voice, because she was still peering into the can. 'It sounds as though he's paddling. Why don't you answer, Calidor?'

There was a splash and a faint mew. John rushed to the watering can and, putting in his hand, lifted out a bedraggled kitten, dripping with dirty water and mewing pitifully.

'You poor little thing!' said Rosemary, trying to wipe off the slime with her nightdress.

But the kitten only whimpered, 'Where's Woppit! Want Woppit!'

'What on earth is Woppit?' asked John.

'Here be old Woppit, my pretty dears!' said a voice behind them, and there in the doorway was a dusty, dishevelled, elderly tabby cat.

'Bother!' said Pergamond crossly.

'As if they could keep old Woppit away! "Too big for a nurse now," they said. But I knows better! Me that's looked after 'em since before their blessed blue eyes was open. They thought they'd hoodwinked old Woppit and whisked you away without her knowing. But I smells here, and I asks there, and sure enough, I've found my little furry sweetings! And where's my precious princeling puss?'

All the time she was talking, Woppit was purring loudly and comfortably. But when she caught sight of Calidor, bedraggled and miserable in Rosemary's lap, her untidy fur bristled with indignation.

'What have the horrid humans been doing to you then, my pet? I knew it all along! I never did hold with humans!'

'We aren't wicked, even if we are humans!' said John indignantly. 'And we didn't do anything!'

'It was Calidor's fault,' said Pergamond virtuously. 'We were hungry, and I only said I thought there might be sardines in the water at the bottom of the can, and he was looking to see, and he fell in. He was only doing this.'

She put her front paws on the rim of the can, and heaving her stumpy hind legs up the side, tried to stand on the rim. John's hand shot out again just in time to stop her from falling in as her brother had done. He set her firmly down on the ground.

'But there weren't any sardines,' said Calidor, who was beginning to revive. 'Only a lot of smelly water.'

He sneezed violently. 'I think I've lost a life,' he went on with gloomy satisfaction. 'You'll catch it when father hears!'

'I'm hungry,' mewed Pergamond. 'I want my breakfast!'

'Regular meals they're used to, like any well brought-up kittens. There's some people takes on a job without so much as knowing the first thing about it.' Woppit looked sourly at John and Rosemary.

'Look here,' said John angrily, 'are you suggesting that Rosie and I aren't capable of looking after a couple of kittens?'

'Well then, which of you is going to lick my little princeling clean? And no licking round the corners, mind!'

'Lick him!' said Rosemary in horror, looking at the kitten's matted fur.

'That's what I said. You'll never get him clean without. Either I licks, or you licks, and if I stays and licks, I stays for good!' said Woppit. 'Which is it to be?'

'I should have thought a bath –' began Rosemary. But at the word 'bath' the kittens set up such a mewing, and Woppit's comforting was so noisy, that the children could not hear themselves speak. They slipped outside the greenhouse and shut the door behind them quite firmly.

'Whew!' said John. 'I'm beginning to see what Carbonel means about the kittens being "high spirited".'

'Look here,' interrupted Rosemary, 'I think we should find Woppit very useful. After all, we can't sit and hold their paws all day long.'

'Yes, but I refuse to have an old tabby cat ordering me around,' said John.

'I don't think she'll try if we make her see that we only want to do our best for the kittens.'

'Perhaps you're right,' said John. 'Suppose I run back upstairs and get them some milk, and you see what you can do with old Woppit.' John ran.

When Rosemary went back into the greenhouse, Woppit was already vigorously licking a sulky Calidor. She eyed Rosemary suspiciously, but she did not stop.

'Please, Woppit,' said Rosemary humbly, 'John and I want you to stay and show us how to look after Prince Calidor and Princess Pergamond, if you will.'

With a practised paw, Woppit rolled over a protesting Calidor and went on licking. She said nothing, but there was the faint suggestion of a purr.

'Please, Woppit!' pleaded Rosemary.

'I'll think about it!' said Woppit, as though it were a perfectly new idea of Rosemary's. 'I might do it, to oblige.' But she went on licking the unhappy Calidor so vigorously that Rosemary felt quite sorry for him, and her purring settled down to a deep, contented hum.

At that moment, John burst in at the door. 'Here's some milk, but I only just got out without being seen,' he said. 'I could hear your mother getting up. We'd better hurry.'

They put the saucer down, left Woppit in charge, closed the door of the greenhouse firmly and ran back to the house and breakfast.

7

Figg's Bottom

'REALLY, Rosie,' said Mrs Brown. 'It was naughty of you to say you would look after three cats without asking first!'

Breakfast had been reduced to eggshells and toast crumbs before they had brought up the subject.

'I know, Mummy, I'm awfully sorry, but—'

'It wasn't Rosie's fault,' broke in John. 'You see, the . . . the . . . person they belong to had to go away this morning urgently, and there wasn't time.'

'But *three* cats, dears!'

'One cat and two kittens,' pleaded Rosemary. 'And if you would only come and see them, Mummy, you couldn't say no!'

Mrs Brown tried to go on frowning, but the two pleading faces were too much for her, and presently she smiled.

'All right,' she said at last. 'But if you want to keep them in the greenhouse, you must ask Mr Featherstone's permission, and you must look after them yourselves.'

'Of course we'll look after them, won't we, John? They are very special kittens, and we wouldn't trust them to anyone else. May we go and ask permission this minute?'

The children ran downstairs to the ground floor flat, where they found Mr Featherstone shaving. When he heard them come in, he wheeled round, his razor buzzing in his hand like a wasp in a jam jar.

'Good heavens, it's young John! Rosemary told me you were coming. Glad to see you, my boy! Have a bull's eye. You'll find them somewhere about, on the bookcase I think. I'm afraid it's a bit untidy.'

Rosemary felt that 'untidy' hardly described it. They couldn't find the bull's eyes among the litter of things on the bookcase, but they ran them to earth at last behind the coal scuttle in a very sticky bag. Because of the bull's eyes they explained the situation rather indistinctly. However, Mr Featherstone seemed to understand.

'Three cats in the greenhouse?' he said. 'I don't see why not. No geraniums, so why not kittens? I remember you always had a weakness for the creatures, Rosie. Listen, I've got to take the van into Broomhurst this afternoon. Suppose you and John come with me. I could drop you in the country at the end of the town somewhere, and pick you up on the way back. What do you say?'

John and Rosemary thought it was an excellent idea.

They spent the morning making the greenhouse comfortable for the kittens. Mrs Brown found them an old blanket and the lid of a cardboard box so that they could make a bed. They stacked the old flower pots in a corner and swept the floor and dusted the shelves, to the indignation of a number of spiders and several wood lice. Woppit lay in the sun outside and slept, and the two kittens chased the broom and their own tails, until they, too, fell asleep.

'I expect Blandamour will come to see them soon, and I should like it all to look its very nicest,' said Rosemary, standing back to admire the effect.

'Bless you, she wouldn't notice!' said Woppit from

the doorway. 'Them as lives in high places thinks high and is above such things. Not that it isn't right and proper for the humble likes of you and me to do our best, for all that!'

John did not much care for being bracketed with Woppit as 'humble,' but, luckily, at that moment Mrs Brown arrived.

'I thought that you and the cats might like some milk, and besides I want to be introduced,' she said, setting down a tray. On it were two mugs, a saucer and a jug of milk.

'The black one is Calidor and the other is Pergamond,' said Rosemary, squatting down beside the ball that was two sleeping kittens.

'The little dears!' said her mother softly, stirring them gently with the toe of her shoe. Then she said, 'I've got a picnic tea ready for you. I wanted to make some for Mr Featherstone – I'm sure he doesn't look after himself properly – but he said he would get some in Broomhurst. If you ask him to put you down by the turning to Figg's Bottom, you can go to Turley's Farm and ask for some milk instead of carrying something to drink with you.'

'Do you mean where we went last year after we picked wild daffodils, Mummy?' asked Rosemary.

'That's it. I'm afraid the daffodil field has been built over now. There's a new housing estate, but I think the farm is still there.'

'It be!' said Woppit unexpectedly, though of course only the children heard her. 'I ought to know, seeing as my brother Tudge took on Turleys four years ago.'

When Mrs Brown had gone and both children and kittens were drinking their milk, she went on, 'Ah, if you should meet a cat with a torn ear and a walleye, it'll be Tudge, sure enough. You can tell him he can come and see me if he likes,' she went on graciously. 'I dare say I shall be glad of a bit of company here.'

She looked rather disdainfully around the greenhouse as she spoke.

'What colour is he?' asked John.

'Not to say one colour,' said Woppit cautiously, 'but a bit of most.'

'We'll look out for him,' said Rosemary gravely.

'I'll pick you up about half past five,' said Mr Featherstone, as they rattled cheerfully along in the van.

They passed the familiar outskirts of Fallowhithe and found themselves in the newly built housing estate. They passed the finished houses with new curtains at the windows and new babies asleep in new prams in the front gardens, and were soon in a road with half-built houses on either side.

'Where shall we meet you?' asked John.

'The corner by the Figg's Bottom signpost is as good a meeting place as any. It should be just around the bend when we leave the houses behind,' said Mr Featherstone. But they did not leave the houses behind. A tide of new buildings seemed to be coming toward them.

'Good heavens!' said Mr Featherstone. 'I'd no idea the Broomhurst houses had spread so far.'

'It looks as though a couple more houses will join it up with Fallowhithe,' said John.

Even as they looked, they saw a man pushing a wheelbarrow full of bricks along a plank over the remaining piece of open land, which they saw had the forlorn, naked look of all building sites before the work actually begins.

'Anyway, there are still fields behind the houses on either side,' said John.

The van slowed down and stopped at a turning which still had a country-lane look about it. There was a signpost at the corner which said: TO FIGG'S BOTTOM. The children got out.

John carried their tea in a knapsack. 'We'll be waiting for you, and thank you for bringing us, sir!' he said.

'Enjoy yourselves!' called Mr Featherstone as he let in the clutch, and they watched the van rattle off down the road.

John and Rosemary wandered off to the nearest half-built house and watched a man with no shirt and a very brown back carry a load of bricks up a ladder, and come down again with the empty hod. He stopped at the bottom.

'Can you tell us if the houses will join up in the end?' asked Rosemary. 'I mean so that Fallowhithe and Broomhurst meet?'

The man looked up from his rolling. 'Hello!' he said. 'When we've finished they'll join so neat as you won't know where one begins and the other ends! It makes you think, don't it?'

John agreed that it did.

'If you ask me, the cats have moved in already,' the man went on. 'I've never seen so many. All over the place, they are!'

Even as he spoke, a great black animal with white paws padded silently along the half-built wall, gave them a searching look and disappeared the way it had come.

The man frowned. 'And it's a funny thing,' he went on, 'but there's a rubbish dump here already, even before anyone's moved in. Beats me where it comes from. There's even an old rocking chair.' He jabbed his thumb over his shoulder.

'Hey, Charlie!' shouted a voice.

'Okay, I'm coming,' replied the man. 'So long!' he said. He winked cheerfully at Rosemary and went off whistling.

John and Rosemary turned and wandered off in the direction he had pointed with his thumb. In a field, beyond a cement mixer, was a pile of old tins and some worn-out shoes, and beside it stood a rocking chair.

'I wonder who put it there?' said Rosemary. 'It doesn't look broken to me.'

'Oh, never mind,' said John impatiently. 'We haven't come all this way to examine old rubbish heaps! I'm hungry. I vote we go on down the lane and have our tea as soon as we find a good place. We can go on to Turley's afterwards and get some milk.'

So they turned down the lane leading to Figg's Bottom, but as it happened they never reached Turley's Farm. They walked on in a leisurely way. With nothing but the winding road ahead and fields on either side, it was easy to forget the building behind them They stopped to listen to two sparrows gossiping on the hedge. A snail was making rude remarks to a blackbird from the safety of an overhanging stone. Once a rabbit popped its head through the bars of a stile.

'Humans!' it said in disgust, and popped back again. John stood on the stile to call to it, but said instead, 'I'm sure I can hear a stream. Let's go and find it.' So they crossed the stile and followed a path through the meadow on the other side.

They found the stream without much difficulty. Its clear, cider-coloured water rippled gently over a pebbly bed. They took off their shoes and splashed about happily. Rosemary picked a bunch of water forget-me-nots and wild peppermint. They tried to dam a tiny tributary and let the piled-up water join the main stream again with a whoosh!

It was not till some time later, with toes and fingers very pink and crinkly, that they sat down in the middle of a little plank bridge. With their legs dangling, they ate tomato sandwiches and homemade rock cakes. They were facing upstream, and, when they had nearly finished, John said suddenly, 'Someone must be sailing toy boats higher up! Look, there's a big one just coming round the corner.'

There certainly was a black thing, which looked like a toy boat, drifting toward them.

'Let's catch it when it gets to the bridge!' said Rosemary.

They lowered themselves down into the stream in readiness. But it was not a boat. It was a shoe, a very large one with a brass buckle that needed sewing on again. They caught it as it drifted under the bridge.

'Let's go upstream and see if we can find the owner. Whoever owns it must have enormous feet!' said John.

They lifted the dripping shoe out of the water and started to wade upstream.

8

The Rocking Chair

THEY splashed their way along very pleasantly for some distance, until, coming out of a green tunnel made by the overhanging branches of willow and hazel, they were startled to find themselves in the sunshine again, and almost on top of the owner of the shoe.

'Mrs Cantrip!' said John and Rosemary together. For that is who it was. She was sitting on a rock with the remaining shoe beside her and with her large feet dangling in the water. Beside her, a little higher up the bank, was a small, neat, plump person. She had round cheeks, she wore a round felt hat and a neat tweed suit, and she sat very upright, with a bunch of what looked like green leaves in her lap.

'It's you, is it?' said Mrs Cantrip sourly.

'We rescued your shoe for you,' said John politely, holding it out to her. 'It was floating downstream.'

'Interfering again!' said the old woman. 'It was floating lovely!'

'But we thought whoever it belonged to would want it back,' said John in surprise.

'And we didn't even know it was yours,' added Rosemary. 'You couldn't get home without it.'

'That's all you know. There's more ways of getting about than walking,' said Mrs Cantrip. 'Besides, I know where there's another lovely pair of shoes for the taking, and no questions asked.'

The little person leaned forward and said eagerly, 'If you mean the ones on the rubbish heap where we left the –' She broke off suddenly and clapped her hand over her mouth.

At the same time, Mrs Cantrip deliberately threw her other shoe into the stream with a loud splash. 'You can fish that out, as you're so fond of finding things,' she said rudely.

Red with annoyance, John splashed over and pulled out the second shoe.

'I think you are very ungrateful!' said Rosemary hotly.

'It was entirely my fault, dears!' said the round-about person. 'I'm sure Katie is very grateful, really. Such a character! She was trying to stop me saying something when she threw her shoe into the stream. My foolish tongue, you know.' Then, turning to Mrs Cantrip, 'Such nicely spoken children. Do introduce me, please, Katie dear!'

Mrs Cantrip sniffed.

'Boy nuisance!' she said, nodding toward John. 'And girl nuisance!'

Rosemary turned her back on Mrs Cantrip and said, 'I'm Rosemary, this is my friend John, and we aren't a nuisance, at least not on purpose.'

'And my name is Dibdin,' said the little person, 'Miss Dorothy Dibdin.'

'You aren't Mrs Cantrip's new lodger, are you?' asked Rosemary suddenly.

'Why, how clever of you!' said Miss Dibdin warily. 'Just for the summer holidays, you know. Between you and me, it's not very comfortable, but it has its advantages. It was such a stroke of luck finding it. I always like to have a hobby during the summer holidays – I am a schoolteacher, you know – and Mrs Cantrip is teaching me to –'

She broke off again as Mrs Cantrip burst into a very

loud, artificial cough. 'There I go again,' she continued. 'But no harm done. Such a lovely day! We came here to enjoy the country, to meet some friends and pick a bunch of flowers. You promised to show me where I could find that particularly damaging dodder, dear,' she said to Mrs Cantrip, and at the same time she rose to her feet and dusted her skirt.

Mrs Cantrip grunted, but she heaved herself up, pushed her bare feet into her wet shoes with complete unconcern, and muttering something about 'Bogshott Wood', started to climb the bank, with her shoes squelching at every step.

'Good afternoon, children,' said Miss Dibdin briskly, and followed her up the bank.

'Exactly as though we were six-year-olds,' said John, as they watched the two cross the field, the one so tall and untidy and the other so short and trim.

'Whatever can Mrs Cantrip be teaching her?' said Rosemary.

'Search me,' said John. 'But you can bet she's up to no good. Well, it's nothing to do with us. Come on. We've left our picnic things and shoes by the bridge.'

Since they had reached the bridge earlier in the afternoon, all the little animal voices had been hidden by the chuckling of the stream. Standing on the top of the bank, they became aware of a bird sitting on a swaying twig and calling, 'No good! No good!'

'Do you mean Mrs Cantrip?' asked Rosemary.

'Ugly pair! Ugly pair!' sang the bird. Then, with a frightened whirr of wings, it darted off, just as a cat came dashing down the field with three others in hot pursuit. The frightened animal found himself in the loop of the stream. He paused, looking for some way to cross, but the hesitation lost him the advantage, and his pursuers were upon him. With a yowl and a screech, what had been four cats became one threshing, rolling ball.

'The poor thing!' cried Rosemary in distress. 'It's three against one! The great cowards! Oh, do be careful, John!' she said, for John had taken off his coat, and with some idea of protecting his hands, flung it over the spitting threshing animals.

Whether it was the coat that was responsible or not, the rolling cats, who had been steering a zigzag course toward the stream, reached the edge of the bank, and cats, coat and all bounced down the bank and fell into the water with a splash. There was a screech from all four animals. Then three of them scrambled out and, even faster than they had come, dashed away in the direction of the road, leaving a trail of wet grass behind. The fourth cat stood shivering on the bank. John and Rosemary ran toward him.

'You poor thing!' said Rosemary.

'Let's rub him with my blazer,' said John. 'It's so wet already that more water won't hurt! Keep still old chap!'

'Thank you kindly,' said the cat, through the folds of John's blazer. 'If there's one thing I can't abide, it's water.' An untidy head emerged from the navy-blue flannel. 'Me that was ship's cat for two years on the *Mary Jane*. Trawling, she was.'

John interrupted. 'Rosie! A walleye and a torn ear!' He stood up with the coat in his hands. 'And not one colour, but a bit of most! You must be Tudge!'

The strange cat shook his wet paws in turn. 'What if I be? Personal remarks is rude!'

'I'm sorry!' said John. 'But Woppit told us about you.'

'Her,' said Tudge with great scorn. 'So high and mighty since she took up with royalty, she is, I wonder she still remembers me.'

'Oh, but she does!' said Rosemary. 'She asked us to give you a message if we met you. She said you could come and see her if you liked, and we should love you to. You see, she is helping us look after the two royal kittens. Why, what's the matter?'

The cat looked furtively around and beckoned them down to the water's edge.

'It do be safer to talk here, though damp to the paws. The water makes such a swirligiggle we aren't like to be overheard by them as means them precious kitlings no good. Listen here. For why do you think I were being chased, like as if I'd been caught with cream on my paws in the dairy?'

Tudge did not wait for them to answer. 'Me, Turley's cat on Turley's land, going about my lawful business! I'll tell you for why. Because I challenged them Broomhurst animals, polite but firm, as is my job. Talking they was, to two more hearing humans.'

'Hearing humans?'

'Them as hears us animals talking, like you, of course. And I didn't like the look of them two, neither. One tall, thin and untidy as a scarecrow, and the other round and plump, like a cat full of cream.'

John and Rosemary looked at one another.

'Did you hear what they were talking about?' asked John.

'Well, I'm not a one to go poking into other people's affairs. But as I comes up, the plump one says, "How thrilling! Do let's go!" and claps her hands, and the skinny one says, "We may as well see what she's up to!" And then one of them cats ups and says, "Her Royal

Greyness says you must be there by midnight, and not a word to anyone." "But how would we get there?" says Roundabout. "The way we came here of course!" says Skinny, sharp like. And then they sees me standing there, and I'd barely given the usual challenge when them animals were on me.'

'Did you hear anything else?' asked John.

'Only Skinny cackling and Roundabout saying, "Dear me, dear me." Then I broke away and she called after 'em, "Tell Her Royal Greyness we'll be there!" and she cackled again. You know the rest, thanking you kindly,' said Tudge.

'What do you think they were talking about?' said John curiously. 'And who is Her Royal Greyness?'

'Grisana, Queen of the Broomhurst cats, smoke-grey she is, and a proper fierce one, although she seems so gentle. Not like our lovely Blandamour. But when the Kings get the Summons, it's the Queens who reign till they come home. It's my belief there's mischief brewing. So cook-a-hoop them Broomhurst animals is. Singing rude songs and shouting insults at honest, workaday Fallowhithe animals. When the last house goes up, then look out for trouble!'

'What do you mean?' Rosemary asked.

'I think I know,' said John. 'You mean when the last house is built that joins Broomhurst with Fallowhithe.'

'Ah,' said Tudge. 'No dividing line between the two there won't be. And with King Castrum off to the Summoning, and no one to keep them Broomhurst cats in order, or his Queen who's left in charge, there'll be trouble right enough.'

'Good Heavens!' said John. 'Listen, Tudge, if you hear anything more, will you let us know?'

'I will!' promised Tudge. 'And guard them precious kitlings as if they were gold. You can't be too careful!'

'Oh dear!' said John. 'I wish we hadn't left them for so long.'

'Don't you think we ought to be going?' said Rosemary anxiously.

'Bother! My watch has stopped,' said John. 'I think I've got it wet. We musn't be late for Mr Featherstone. We have to get our shoes from the bridge. Let's get going.'   *   *   *

John and Rosemary said good-bye to Tudge and splashed their way back to the little bridge. As soon as they found their shoes, they hurried back to the signpost, but there was no sign of Mr Featherstone.

The builders had finished for the day and gone home, so they examined a half-built house and tried to imagine it being lived in.

'Let's go and look at the cement mixer,' said John, so they went into the field. John found the cement mixer enthralling, but to Rosemary it was rather dull, so she wandered off, and found herself by the rubbish heap once again.

'I can't see Mrs Cantrip in any of those shoes,' she thought. 'Not with high heels and open toes.' Then she looked at the rocking chair which was still standing beside it. 'I wonder who left it here?' she said to herself.

She rocked it idly with one toe. It did not seem broken, so she sat on the seat. She began rocking gently to and fro. It made a pleasant little breeze, and she went a little higher. As she rocked rhythmically to and fro, she said idly, 'Rocking chair, rocking chair,' in time to the movement, and then thinking a little

anxiously about the kittens, added, 'I wish I was home.
I wish I was there. Oh, that rhymes!'
And she said again, in time to the rocking,

> *'Rocking chair, rocking chair.*
> *I wish I was home, I wish I was there!'*

And because the chant went so well with the movement
of the chair, she said it a third time, rocking higher
and higher, and then she gave the chair a tremendous
push forward.

To her complete surprise, the chair rose steeply into
the air, then banked sharply, nearly throwing her out.
She held on firmly, too astonished to call out.

Down below, John suddenly looked up and saw
Rosemary, her feet curled around the front legs of
the rocking chair and plaits flapping wildly. The chair
righted itself and seemed to be flying steadily in the
direction of Fallowhithe. He thought he saw her lips
moving as she turned to look back at him, but he was
too far away to hear what she was saying. But he
saw her point behind him toward Figg's Bottom.

'Rosie, come back!' he called, although he knew it
was useless. He ran desperately in the direction the
chair was taking, with some wild idea of keeping pace
with it. But when he turned to look where Rosemary
was pointing he stopped dead.

Mrs Cantrip and Miss Dibdin were panting up the
hill from Figg's Bottom. They looked up at the disappearing chair and waved angrily.

'Stop thief! Stop thief!' called Miss Dibdin shrilly.

They had not seen John, so he slipped back to the
half-built house, and hid in what was going to be the
kitchen. He held his breath as the hurrying feet came
near. He could distinguish the flap, flap of Mrs

Cantrip's shoes and the click, click of Miss Dibdin's neat, high heels. As they drew level with his hiding place, the footsteps stopped.

'You must wait a minute, Katie. I've got a stone in my shoe, and if you think I'm going to run all the way home to Fairfax Market, you're very much mistaken,' Miss Dibdin said tartly. 'You must admit it's a pretty how-do-you-do. No rocking chair to take us home and no money for a bus, thanks to your saying witches don't carry handbags.'

'It's them children again, I'm sure of it!' growled Mrs Cantrip. 'I knew there'd be trouble the minute I set eyes on 'em.'

John could hear the sound of an approaching car,

but did not dare to look up to see if it was Mr Feather-stone.

'And now how are we to get there tomorrow night, I should like to know?' Miss Dibdin asked. 'The highest building in Broomhurst you said it was. We shall just have to hurry up with that broom. Oh, I know you can't do anything, but you can tell me how to finish it.'

'What, both of us ride tandem on a young broom that's not been broken in?' said Mrs Cantrip. 'Mad-ness, I call it! You'd ruin its temper for life. But we'll get there somehow, if it's only to get even with those children. Not that it isn't as nice a bit of mischief as

I've seen in a month of wet Mondays. Don't be all day with that shoe!'

'Well, I suppose there's nothing for it,' said Miss Dibdin briskly. 'We shall just have to walk the six miles home. You can teach me that handy little spell for turning milk sour as we go.'

As John listened to their retreating footsteps, a car passed his hiding place and drew up a little farther on. He looked cautiously over the wall. The two women had started off at a rapid pace. He saw with relief that Mr Featherstone was standing by the van.

'Hello!' he said. 'Where's Rosie? Had a good time?'

'Super!' said John. 'Rosie . . . er . . . was given a lift home by someone she knows,' he said lamely.

'Really? How very strange of her,' said Mr Featherstone in a puzzled voice. 'Have you two had a row? You sound rather gloomy. Well, if she gets back safely I suppose that's all that matters.'

John most heartily agreed.

It was a silent drive home. John was far too busy with his thoughts for conversation. Quite clearly, Mrs Cantrip, although she had retired from being a witch herself, was instructing Miss Dibdin, and both of them were planning mischief with the cats of Broomhurst. Worse still was his anxiety about Rosemary.

When they reached home, John thanked Mr Featherstone and rushed to the greenhouse to see if the kittens were safe. He burst in at the door.

'Are they safe, Woppit?' he asked. 'The kittens, I mean?'

'They're safe enough,' said Woppit.

'Look here, no matter what happens don't let them out of your sight for a minute,' said John. 'There may be trouble brewing. 'I'll come and explain as soon as I can, but I must go now. I know I can trust you!'

'Trust me?' said Woppit indignantly. 'And who better, I'd like to know. To the last whisker!'

9

The Walled Garden

ROSEMARY had seen Mrs Cantrip and Miss Dibdin
burst into a run when they caught sight of the rocking chair climbing steeply into the air, but when she
saw John hide himself in the half-built house, she gave
a sigh of relief. It gave her something else to think
about besides the dizzy feeling in her head and the
sudden emptiness of her inside.

'This must have been what Mrs Cantrip meant
when she said, "There's other ways than walking."'
Rosemary said to herself. 'I don't expect I've anything
to be frightened about,' she went on severely, taking a
firm grip of the arms of the chair. 'I suppose because I
said "I wish I was home," and three times, too, that's
where the chair is taking me. How surprised Mum
will be!'

By this time, she could bring herself to look down
without feeling giddy. Behind, she could see the tip of
the pink wedge that was the new houses leading from
Broomhurst, and the thought that John was there
gave her courage. Suddenly, roofs and chimneys swirled
and dipped beneath her. Few people looked up, but
those who did scarcely had time to rub their eyes and
look again before the rocking chair was too far away to
be distinguished.

The chair flew over the railway station where, such
a short time ago, Rosemary and her mother had met
John. A curious swallow swooped alongside. 'Flying

humans! What next?' it said, and swooped away again.

Then, Rosemary noticed with alarm that the chair was losing height. 'My goodness, we're going down! Chair do be careful!'

The rows of crooked chimneys seemed to be coming straight up at her. She shut her eyes tightly, but even so, she, had a sinking, going-down-in-a-lift feeling. Then there was a violent bump, and the chair overturned, throwing her in a heap on to a patch of long grass. She opened her eyes and sat up, surprised to find that, except for a few bruises, she was none the worse for her fall. She looked around cautiously.

She was in a little garden. It was very small and surrounded on three sides by a high wall, with broken glass along the top. The fourth side was the back of a very shabby, small house. She got up and looked at the flower beds which ran around the little patch of grass. 'It's a very strange garden!' Rosemary said. It was very neat, but there were no flowers, as she knew them.

'Somebody has actually been growing weeds on purpose!' There was a clump of stinging nettles carefully staked and tied, and another of hemlock, and there was a neat edging of dandelions. There were a great many plants that Rosemary did not recognize, nearly all of them with small, greenish flowers.

'That bush is deadly nightshade! I know it is, because the berries are poisonous, and someone has put a net over it to keep off the birds, just as you do with raspberries!' There was a clumsy garden seat made from packing cases. A seed box stood beside it with a label which said, MANDRAKE SEEDLINGS. SPARRERS KEEP OFF.

Rosemary watched a bee back clumsily out of a foxglove bell, and for the first time noticed the hum of a small thatched beehive. It stood in an angle of the garden wall. The bee hummed a little song which sounded like this:

> 'Busycum, buzzycum,
> Nectar and honeycomb.
> Lilac and lime on the tree,
> Roses and lilies
> And daffydown dillies,
> Are not for the likes of me.
> Not for a witch's bee!'

'Excuse me,' said Rosemary, 'but can you tell me whose garden this is?'

The bee took no notice, but buzzing busily, pushed itself into the next foxglove bell. When it backed out again, it went on humming its song as though she had not spoken.

> 'Busycum, buzzycum,
> Pains in the tummy cum,
> Sowthistle, poisonous pea,
> Henbane and hellebore,
> That's what I'm looking for,
> That's for the likes of me,
> Food for a witch's bee!'

'Of course I do like your song, but *please* tell me where I am!' said Rosemary once more.

The bee stood on the lip of the foxglove bell, which dipped with its weight, and paused to clean its back legs.

'A hearing human, eh?' it said. 'I've heard of 'em of course, but never met one before. Full of surprises, this garden is. Whose is it? That'd be telling. Where are you? Where you'd much better not be!' And it boomed off, still humming to itself, 'Busycum, buzzycum.'

'Oh, dear!' said Rosemary. 'That's not much help. I expect I had better knock at the door. It's going to be awfully difficult to explain how I got here.'

She tiptoed up to what was clearly the back door of the house and knocked. While she was waiting for an answer, she looked through the window beside it. There was a window box on the sill, full of brightly coloured toadstools. The room inside looked unpleasantly familiar. There was still no answer, so she tried the door and, finding it unlocked, tiptoed in.

'Oh, dear!' said Rosemary for a third time. 'It *is* Mrs Cantrip's kitchen! How silly I have been! When I said "home," the rocking chair took me to the only one it knew!

'Is there anyone here?' she called in a rather wobbly voice. There was no answer. 'Well, there couldn't be,' she said with relief, 'because it will take them a long time to walk all the way back from Figg's Bottom.'

Rosemary looked around the kitchen curiously. It was much the same as the last time she had seen it. It was quite tidy. The hearth was swept and the fire banked up. Dandelions, which had decorated the table, had been changed for a bunch of dead nettles. On the rag rug by the hearth lay a long wooden stick and a pile of twigs. Then her eyes were caught by a small cupboard hanging on the wall by the fireplace.

The door was open, so she went over and looked in. On the top shelf were sugar and tea, cornflakes and nutmeg, and all the usual things found in a kitchen cupboard. But a screw of paper caught Rosemary's eye on the lower shelf. 'It looks like the Prism Powder Mrs Cantrip left in her apron pocket.'

Next to it was an old tin, which had a label gummed crookedly onto the side which said, DISAPPEARING POTION, but it was empty. Next to that was a jam jar with some purple liquid at the bottom, labelled FLYING PHILTRE, USE SPARINGLY, and beside that was a pickle jar with a few grains of coarse powder at the bottom. The label on this said MINUSCULE MAGIC.

'So Mrs Cantrip really did have some magic left over!' said Rosemary.

As she spoke, she heard the Market Hall clock strike six o'clock. 'I must start home. It will take me ages to walk to Cranshaw Road!' She went through to the second room which opened onto the street and tried the door. To her horror it was locked! There was no key to be seen.

'I expect Mrs Cantrip has taken it with her. Whatever shall I do?' She ran to the window which looked onto the street, but it had been built as a shop window and it did not open. She walked back to the kitchen slowly as the situation dawned on her. There was no way out, and at any minute Mrs Cantrip and her companion might be back.

She looked out of the kitchen window which opened onto the little garden. The rocking chair was on the small square of grass. It looked rather forlorn, lying on its side by the skid marks it had made when it landed.

Rosemary ran out. She picked it up and dusted it with her handkerchief. 'Rocking chair,' she pleaded, 'it was very clever of you to bring me here. I expect it is your home, but I want desperately to get to *my* home in Cranshaw Road. Please, will you take me there now? If you will, I'll polish you up so beautifully that the Queen herself would be proud to sit in you!'

She was not sure if she imagined it, but she thought the chair gave a faint rock of its own accord.

'Now I'll try and do just what I did before. I said a rhyme, I remember, three times over, and all the while I was rocking.'

Rosemary sat herself in the chair and put her hands over her eyes to help her think, and began to rock. It was a little while before she could make her whirling thoughts obey her. 'It's not a very good rhyme,' she said at last, 'but it will have to do. I can't think of a better one.'

Anyone who has had to make up a rhyme with the words 'one hundred and one' in it, will realize her difficulty. She rocked the chair steadily, and at last she gripped the arms firmly and said:

> *'Please take me home to Cranshaw Road.*
> *One hundred and one is my abode.*
> *My bedroom window's open wide,*
> *So kindly take me right inside.'*

As she got to the last line, she heard footsteps coming along the pavement on the other side of the wall. It sounded like two people, both of them limping a little.

'It's Mrs Cantrip! Someone must have given them a lift!' said Rosemary to herself. 'I must hurry!'

She rocked higher and faster, saying the rhyme for a second time. As she reached the last line, she heard a key grating in the lock. It made such a noise that it was clearly as large as a church key. The lock needed oiling.

She said the last line for the third time, and just as

the door opened on its creaking hinges, the rocking chair rose from the ground with a swoop, spiralling steeply. She was just wondering if she ought to have added the postal number to the address when it straightened out. She opened her eyes and looked down. Already the little walled garden was no bigger than a green pocket handkerchief beneath her. Straight as an arrow, the chair headed for Cranshaw Road.

Making Plans

JOHN and Mrs Brown ate a silent, uncomfortable supper by themselves. He was a truthful boy and, being unable to think of anything better to say, repeated his story of someone having given Rosemary an unexpected lift. The unexpected part was certainly true.

'But who could it have been?' asked Mrs Brown anxiously for the tenth time. 'It's so unlike Rosemary!' She broke off, to John's intense relief, startled by a crash from Rosemary's bedroom. The room was not much larger than a cupboard, and its only door led into the sitting room. John dropped his pudding spoon and rushed in.

As Rosemary said later, the rocking chair was 'willing but not very good at landing.' When John flung the door open, the chair was lying on its side, and Rosemary, looking slightly dazed, was picking herself up from the floor. With great presence of mind, he pushed the chair behind the door, and stood so that, as far as possible, it was hidden from Mrs Brown. Then, winking violently in an effort to convey that she had better think up something quickly, he said loudly, 'Hello, Rosie!'

For once Mrs Brown was extremely cross.

'Rosemary! You are a very naughty girl! I can't think why you should do something so childish as to hide in your bedroom while I have been so anxious.

And what possessed you to leave Mr Featherstone and come home with someone else?'

'I'm very sorry, Mummy,' said Rosemary penitently. 'I really didn't mean you to be anxious. It was all a mistake, honestly. I promise I won't ever do it again. Please, just this once,' she went on earnestly, 'will you trust me and not ask questions? It is a most particular secret!'

Mrs Brown looked at her daughter's pleading face for an anxious moment. Then at last she said, 'You promise the secret is not wrong?'

'Promise faithfully!' said Rosemary.

'Very well, dear. I will trust you. But you must not be inconsiderate either. You have been rude to Mr Featherstone as well as making me anxious. But come and have your supper now, Rosie. It's in the oven. You must be starving.'

'Are the kittens all right?' asked Rosemary, between mouthfuls of fish pie.

'Right as rain,' said John. 'But I think we ought to feed them as soon as possible,' he went on, winking violently again, hoping that Rosemary would understand that he wanted to talk to her privately.

They had to help wash up after supper, but as soon as the door closed behind them, Rosemary told John her adventures. He listened open-mouthed.

'I was in such a tizzy to get away from Mrs Cantrip's garden that I forgot I wouldn't be able to explain how I came to be in my bedroom without going through the sitting room. We shall have to think of some way to hide the chair, or Mother will want to know where it came from.'

'Smuggle it down to the Green Cave for the moment,

and cover it with leaves,' John suggested. 'But *I've* got
something to tell *you*!'

When John described the conversation he had overheard when he was hiding in the half-built house, it
was Rosemary's turn to be impressed.

'Thank goodness they didn't catch you!' she said.
'Well, it's quite clear that Mrs Cantrip and that Dibdin woman are hatching some plot with the Queen of
the Broomhurst cats. Tudge said that trouble was
brewing.'

'And he thought it was against Fallowhithe!'

'If they're meeting tomorrow night on top of the
tallest building in Broomhurst, it must be on that
new ten-storey block of offices that Mr Featherstone
told us about. I'd give my boots for us to be behind a
chimney so that we could listen to what they're up
to.'

'John!' said Rosemary excitedly. 'Why shouldn't we
go?'

'But they're meeting in the middle of the night.
How could we get on to the roof? The place would be
locked up!'

'Well,' said Rosemary,' as Mrs Cantrip said, "there's
other ways than walking!"'

John whistled. 'Do you mean the rocking chair?
Do you think it could carry us both?'

'We could ask it in the morning. I think it's had
enough for one day. Come on, let's feed the kittens.'

It was growing dusk when they reached the greenhouse. When they opened the door an unexpected
sight greeted them. Blandamour was sitting on an upturned flower pot, and at her feet were the two kittens,
both sitting up as straight and still as their royal
mother.

Woppit looked on with her head on one side and a doting expression on her brindled face. 'Hush!' she said to John and Rosemary. 'The little darlings is saying their lessons!'

In small, piping voices the kittens were repeating:

> *'No paw or whisker in the dish,*
> *Whether meat or fowl or fish . . .'*

Calidor's voice faltered when a delicious tendril of haddock smell wafted from the plate Rosemary held and tickled his nose.

'Calidor, pay attention!' said Blandamour. 'Each awkward . . .'

The black kitten sighed, but went on:

> *'Each awkward bone be sure to gnaw*
> *Upon the plate, not on the floor.*
> *Lap your milk from out the platter*
> *From the edge, and do not scatter*
> *Drops from either bowl or mug*
> *On quarried floor or silken rug.*
> *Steady lapping, rhythmic, quiet,*
> *Is correct for milky diet.*
> *After food, wash paws and face,*
> *And don't forget to purr your grace.'*

'Very good, my children. Now you may eat,' said Blandamour. 'But remember what you have repeated. Greetings to you, John and Rosemary. My children are well, and if they are closely confined, no doubt you have your reasons!'

'We certainly have, your Majesty!' said John. 'It's like this . . .'

Blandamour listened in silence. Only once did she interrupt to summon a grizzled old tabby cat with four white stockings who was sitting in the shadow of the bushes outside.

'Merbeck, my cousin and chief councillor,' she said. 'He too must hear your tale.'

When the children had finished, she bowed her beautiful white head.

'You have done well and bravely, and I am grateful. But it will need more courage still to fly to Cat Country and overhear Grisana's schemings. It may even be dangerous. Merbeck, should we not send a pair of animals instead?'

Merbeck shook his grizzled head. 'I think not, your Majesty. Grisana is wily in her wickedness. Her sentry will be on the alert for foreign cats, but flying humans they will not expect.'

'Couldn't I go too, oh, couldn't I?' asked Calidor, standing with his short legs spread out and his tail waving angrily. 'I'd show 'em!'

'Me too!' said Pergamond shrilly.

'No, my son,' said Blandamour. 'One day when you are older you will have many chances to prove how brave you are. Until we find out Grisana's plans, we do not know where the danger lies.'

'Therefore, we must go warily and keep our eyes and ears open. Above all, guard the royal kittens!' said Merbeck. 'Tomorrow we will come again and hear what you have discovered, and may good luck go with you!'

11

Cat Country

ROSEMARY kept her promise to the chair the next morning. While John mended the lock of the greenhouse, she carried dusters and furniture polish down to the Green Cave. She rubbed away until her arms ached and the curves of the dark wood of the chair gleamed with little, bright reflections.

'The Queen herself really would be proud to sit in you now, just as I promised,' said Rosemary, sitting back on her heels to admire her handiwork.

The chair gave a little rock which seemed to show it was pleased. Or had she caught it with her duster?

'And I know a real queen who might come and sit in you,' went on Rosemary. There was another little rock. 'A cat queen!'

The rocking stopped abruptly.

'A beautiful, snow-white queen who needs your help,' she went on hurriedly. 'Dear rocking chair, you carried me home so splendidly, won't you help us again? You see –' Once more she explained about the meeting on the tallest building in Broomhurst.

'Roofs and walls are Cat Country at night,' she said. 'The place will be locked. Our only way to get there is by flying, if only you will take us. I'll make you –' she thought quickly – 'an antimacassar! You know, one of those things to hang over the back – an embroidered one. I promise!'

Rosemary held her breath. There was a moment's pause, and then the chair gave another little rock.

'I knew I could rely on you!' she whispered, and ran back to the flat to get her nightdress case. It would make an excellent chair-back, she felt. Armed with needles and coloured thread, she went back to the greenhouse to tell John of her success.

It was beginning to rain. Woppit was asleep in a corner, her untidy whiskers twitching as she chased dream mice around a shadowy dream cellar. The kittens were playing with something that rolled obligingly round the floor, and John was whistling through his teeth and fiddling with the lock which he had taken to pieces.

'Good!' he said absently, when Rosemary told him that she thought the rocking chair would take them.

It was almost cosy in the greenhouse, with the raindrops plopping on the glass roof. They worked away in friendly silence. Rosemary was sewing 'R.C.' for Rocking Chair in green chain stitch on the nightdress case. She looked up and bit off her thread. 'Can you really put it together again?'

John looked with a puzzled frown at the bits of lock which he had laid out on the floor.

'If two screws hadn't vanished into thin air, I could,' he snapped. 'You might try to find them instead of sitting there doing nothing.'

'I've been working twice as hard as you!' said Rosemary. 'I've been making up a flying rhyme for tonight all the time I've been sewing!' But she put down her work and looked for the screws. 'They can't have vanished,' she said. 'Have you seen them, kittens?'

Pergamond and Calidor were staring with deep interest at a curled-up wood louse. They looked up, to the wood louse's relief.

'Screws?' asked Calidor. 'What screws?'

'Do they roll?' asked Pergamond.

Rosemary nodded.

'Then they're down there,' said Calidor, peering through the pierced pattern of the iron grille covering the pipes under the floor which once had warmed the greenhouse.

'We were pretending they were mice,' said Pergamond, 'so they had to go down a hole.'

Both kittens peered down into the darkness. They could see the hot water pipes, but not the screws.

'Come on, Rosie, help me pull up the grille!' said John. They pulled and pulled, but it would not budge.

'Rusted in, I suppose,' said John disgustedly. 'Of all the stupid interfering animals!'

The kittens hung their heads. Rosemary scooped them up and put one on each shoulder. They were so very soft and light! She listened to the quick beating of their hearts.

'Don't be cross with them,' she said, and two small rough tongues rasped her hands gratefully as she lifted them into her lap. 'They didn't mean to be a nuisance. I'll hold them here and keep them out of mischief while you finish.' The kittens sparred drowsily in the hollow of her skirt. John put the lock together again and screwed it to the door. The key turned silently in the newly-oiled works.

'It looks splendid to me!' said Rosemary hopefully.

'My good girl, a lock on the door is not much use without the plate on the doorpost for it to fit into!'

They looked up as footsteps scrunched toward them on the gravel path. It was Mr Featherstone.

'Hello! I thought I would find you here. Well, this makes a very snug little kitten garden. I've been suggesting to your mother that, as it's wet, we might all four of us go to the movies this afternoon. There's a very funny film at the Parthenon, I'm told. What do you say?'

Of course they both said yes.

'Good. Can't stop now, see you later,' said Mr Featherstone, who went whistling down the path. Both John and Rosemary were glad for something to fill in the time before their perilous adventure that night. It seemed to grow more perilous the more they thought about it.

'We can buy a couple more screws on our way home,' said John.

'Come on, it's time we got cleaned up,' said Rosemary, looking at his oily hands. 'We can wedge the door shut till this evening.'

The film was so funny that they saw it twice, quite forgetting about the screws, and when they came blinking out into the daylight with their cheeks still creased with laughter, the shops had closed.

'Well, the door will just have to stay wedged until tomorrow,' said John. 'I expect it'll be all right.'

'I hope so,' said Rosemary anxiously. 'Don't forget, eleven-thirty sharp in my bedroom.'

*   *   *

Rosemary decided to undress as usual that evening. When Mrs Brown came to say good night, she would notice if her daughter's clothes were not folded at the foot of the bed.

'Mother, I do like Mr Featherstone, don't you?' asked Rosemary, as her mother tucked her in. 'It was nice this afternoon when we all had tea together.'

Mrs Brown smoothed the bedspread with unusual care. She laughed, but she did not answer.

'Go to sleep now, poppet,' was all she said as she bent to kiss her daughter good night.

Rosemary was determined to do nothing of the sort. Both she and John had decided that, rather than take the risk of oversleeping, it would be wiser to stay awake. But one minute she was going over the rhyme that she had made up for the flying spell, and the next, John was shaking her by the shoulder.

'Wake up, you owl! It's twenty to twelve!' he whispered.

Rosemary shot up from the bedclothes. 'Why ever didn't you wake me sooner?'

'I couldn't,' said John. 'Your mother was pottering about in the sitting room for ages, so I couldn't get through. And then I had to wait till I was pretty certain she was asleep. You haven't time to dress. Come on, you'll just have to put on your dressing gown.'

Rosemary tied the cord of her old red dressing gown around her waist and pushed her toes into her shoes. Then she picked up the newly embroidered antimacassar.

'Let's go!' she whispered.

The house was full of small night noises as they crept out. Boards creaked and the curtains stirred in a little breeze. Once John fell over a stool, but Mrs Brown did not seem to wake. They tiptoed down the stairs and out into the moonlit garden.

It was strangely transformed by the pale light, with a magic that had nothing to do with Mrs Cantrip and her kind. The familiar back of the house had become a mysterious palace, with gleaming, moon-touched windows. The blues and purples of the garden had disappeared. Only the pale flowers gleamed silver in the strange light. The tobacco plants raised their white trumpets to the sky and, together with the clumps of white stock, filled the air with a heavy perfume. Jasmine starred the shadowy porch, and the Mermaid rose dropped slow, pale petals on the weedy path. A moth fluttered by, sighing something that Rosemary could not quite hear.

'John!' she said. 'Anything could happen on a night like this!'

'Well, I'll tell you what *will* happen if we don't hurry up,' said John. 'We won't get to that roof-top place until the meeting is over. We should look pretty silly turning up there when they've all gone home again.'

He seized Rosemary's hand, and together they ran down the path, in and out of light and shadow.

'It's us, chair! John and me!' called Rosemary softly when they reached the Green Cave.

They dived into the moon-chequered darkness under the currant bushes.

'I've brought it. I promised I would! The anti-macassar, I mean,' said Rosemary. 'I embroidered your initials on it specially,' she said proudly, as she tied it on to the back of the chair with two hair ribbons. The chair seemed to give a pleased little jump as Rosemary fluffed out the bows.

'For goodness' sake!' said John impatiently. 'I bet that rocking chair is a female the way it carries on about its appearance,' he growled. 'No male chair would be so soppy!'

'Hush,' said Rosemary quickly. The chair had stopped rocking abruptly. 'I hope you haven't hurt its feelings.'

John was not listening.

'You sit on the seat,' he said, as they carried it from

the shelter of the bushes and stood it on the garden path. 'I'll stand on the rockers behind and hold on to the back.'

Rosemary opened her mouth to say something, but John said, 'Do hurry! There's no time to argue.'

She sat cautiously in the chair and held firmly on to the arms. It was lucky she did. Neither of them knew quite how it happened, but no sooner had John balanced on the rockers behind her than the chair gave a lurch and overbalanced. Rosemary had not far to fall, but John picked himself up ruefully with a grazed knee.

'I thought you'd offended it!' said Rosemary. 'Do say you're sorry and then we can get on. It must be growing awfully late.'

'Oh, I'm sorry!' growled John. 'I didn't mean to hurt your feelings!'

The chair bridled slightly. John dabbed at his knee with a handkerchief, which even in the moonlight looked grubby. Then, very gingerly, he squashed into the seat beside Rosemary. They could just manage it.

'Now then, we must rock with our feet and hope for the best!' said Rosemary. 'Together! One! Two!' The chair rocked, reluctantly at first, then, as Rosemary repeated the rhyme she had prepared, settled into a steady, swinging motion.

> *'In Broomhurst Town we want to find*
> *The tallest roof, if you don't mind.*
> *We'll sit as quiet as anything,*
> *And ever more your praises sing.'*

Higher and higher swung the chair, and as Rosemary repeated the rhyme for the third time, it rose smoothly from the ground, up into the moon-washed air. It spiralled high above Cranshaw Road, then turned sharply in the direction of Broomhurst.

'Yoicks! Tally ho!' shouted John, bouncing up and down on the seat. 'This is simply super!'

Rosemary's plaits streamed behind with their speed. Below them lay the sleeping town, a huddle of silver roofs. Or were they roofs? The sharp angles of gables and chimneys seemed softened in the moonlight.

'If I didn't know they were roofs I should think they were hills and valleys,' shouted John above the wind.

'So would I!' agreed Rosemary. 'Those moving dots must be cats!'

They were flying high now, following the string of pale green street lights that lit the main road to Broomhurst like a string of precious stones. As if uncertain of its way the chair swooped down, casting uncomfortably this way and that at the edge of the town.

'That's the way!' said John pointing to the left. 'I can see the lane leading to Figg's Bottom, and there are the newly-built houses! That's the one I hid in! Good Heavens, they've built a lot since yesterday! Good old rocking chair!'

The chair had risen sharply again after turning obediently in the direction of John's pointing finger.

'What if we can't find which is the tallest building?' called John. 'We can't measure them!'

Far away, a clock chimed midnight.

'Oh, do hurry, *dear* chair!' said Rosemary, and the chair redoubled its speed.

Fortunately there was no mistaking the tallest building. Until recently, Broomhurst had been a sleepy, old-fashioned little town like Fallowhithe. The coming of new industries had brought new life and new ways. So far, only a small section near the railway stastation had been modernized. There was a department store and a clinic, as well as apartment and office buildings. The old-fashioned roof tops which looked like foothills huddled around the base of the mountainous new buildings, the tallest of which was undoubtedly the office building. A breeze had sprung up, and little clouds were scudding across the face of the moon.

'Bother!' said Rosemary. 'Now we can't see properly!'

'It's not a bad thing really,' said John. 'It may give us more chance of landing without being spotted. The old chair ought to –'

Rosemary nudged him sharply.

He added hastily, 'I mean if the *dear* rocking chair would *kindly* circle around so we can spot a good landing place, when the moon is covered, we could land without being seen. It's after twelve, so Mrs Cantrip will have arrived. Even if they have posted cats as sentries, they will be off their guard because they won't expect anyone else.'

Already the chair was circling the building.

'That looks like a good place!' said John. 'Behind that ventilator shaft. The moon is just going behind a cloud. Now!'

The chair rose sharply, then with a sickening swoop dropped toward the ventilator shaft, which seemed to spin up toward them as they swung down.

'We will make such a clatter when we land that everyone will hear for miles!' thought Rosemary desperately, and she closed her eyes, waiting for the shock.

The chair landed fair and square on its rockers, with a jolt that shook the teeth in their heads. Oddly enough, it was a silent landing. The two children climbed out rather shakily. The rocking chair still swayed slightly, as if it were out of breath. The moonlight flooded the sky once more and illuminated the roof top.

'But these aren't slates and chimneys!' said John looking at the soft grass at his feet. 'I thought this was a ventilator shaft, but it's nothing of the sort. It's a tree!'

'Cat Country!' said Rosemary softly. 'That's what Carbonel called it. Hush! I can hear someone talking!'

12

Conspiracy

JOHN put a restraining hand on Rosemary's arm.

'It may be Cat Country, but they are enemy cats. We can't rush in without spying out the land first!'

Rosemary nodded. Then she turned to the rocking chair.

'Chair, dear! Thank you for bringing us so splendidly!' she whispered.

'Yes, rather!' said John. 'Almost as good as a jet.'

'And much, much more quietly!' added Rosemary quickly. 'Wait for us, chair. I don't think anyone will see you tucked away here. We won't be long, at least I hope not.'

'Come on!' said John. 'Bother, it's gone dark again.'

They waited till the trailing wisp of cloud had drifted across the face of the moon and the silver light flooded out. The tree they had thought was a ventilator shaft seemed to have redoubled its size. The trunk was wide and strong and scored with the claw sharpenings of innumerable cats. Crouching on the little bank where the tree grew, they peered through tall grass and catnip which grew thickly along the top. On the other side, the bank sloped steeply down to a little hollow from which a stream bubbled. It chuckled along, winding and weed-fringed, toward a thicket of slender trees, where it disappeared underground, still talking to itself.

'It doesn't look like water. It's white,' said Rosemary.

But John was not listening. 'If this is Cat Country, it's funny there isn't a cat to be seen!' he said.

'There are the voices again!' whispered Rosemary.

'Cross voices they sound, too!' said John. 'That's where they come from, that little clump of trees. Come on. We'd better not take any risks, even if we can't see any cats. Keep your head down and follow me!'

The ground was broken by low patches of undergrowth. Crouching low, they crept down the bank and made their way in a series of little runs from bush to bush. When they reached the last one large enough to hide behind, they were within easy reach of the trees. Rosemary was just going to stretch her cramped back when John pulled her down again.

'Look at that rock a few feet away!' he breathed. Rosemary looked. On the top, sitting so still that he might have been part of it, was a cat. His eyes were the merest slits of emerald green. As they looked, the slits disappeared altogether. His eyes were closed. At the same time, a second cat leaped up on to the rock beside him. Instantly the green eyes opened wide.

'It's all right, Noggin!' said the first cat hurriedly. 'I was only having a little think, and I can always do it better with my eyes closed.'

'No good sentry *thinks*,' growled Noggin. 'I suppose, like all the others I've just inspected, you were thinking there's no need to keep your eyes open because the Flying Women are here. Well, you're wrong, Swabber! There may be two more about, enemy ones, a Flying Boy and a Flying Girl.' John nudged Rosemary. 'Her Royal Greyness has just sent word.'

'I don't hold with humans in Cat Country,' said Swabber sulkily. 'It's never been done before, and I don't like it.'

'No more than I do,' said Noggin. 'But orders is orders. And if the next sentry is "thinking", I'll pull his whiskers for him!'

Still grumbling, Noggin slipped silently off the rock and loped away across the moonlit grass.

Swabber waited until he was out of sight, and muttering something about 'a lot of fuss', curled up and promptly went to sleep.

'Now!' whispered John with his mouth so close to Rosemary's ear that it tickled.

They crept from the shadow of the bush, thankful for the covering noise of the little stream, and once around the rock they ran to the shelter of the thicket. Just as they reached it, Rosemary stumbled.

'Ow!' she exclaimed.

'Shut up!' hissed John.

'It's all very well!' whispered Rosemary indignantly, hopping up and down and holding her shin. 'I stepped on something crackly, and it bit me!'

They looked down. There on the grass was a broom. It was made from a bundle of twigs bound onto a handle, the sort that is used by gardeners – and witches. It was tethered to one of the little trees.

'It must be the new broom Miss Dibdin made, and they must have both ridden on it after all!' said Rosemary.

The voices sounded very close now. John and Rosemary crept from tree to tree, hardly daring to breathe, until John put out a warning hand. Looking over his shoulder, Rosemary saw a small open space in the middle of the thicket. In the centre was a tree stump, and on it sat what was clearly Her Royal Greyness. She was a beautiful, grey Persian cat with brilliant green eyes. There were several other animals grouped

around her, sitting among the plants which grew thickly in the little clearing. The green eyes turned restlessly from one to the other of the two women seated on a low rock in front of her.

Mrs Cantrip and Miss Dibdin, quite undisturbed by their royal company, were arguing hotly. Mrs Cantrip had lost a shoe again, and her lank hair had escaped from the very large pins which usually kept it fairly tidy, but she seemed quite unruffled. Miss Dibdin, on the other hand, was clearly in a bad temper. Her hat was crooked and her trim suit was rumpled and untidy. While the children watched, she took off her hat and tried to readjust her bun.

'If you didn't enjoy it, it's your own fault,' Mrs Cantrip was saying. 'You would come, though I warned you, and you made the broom yourself, so I don't see you've anything to grumble about. As I told you, it takes years to train a broomstick to fly smooth and obedient with only one person up, let alone two!'

Miss Dibdin muttered something indistinctly because her mouth was full of hairpins.

'Ah, I've known some broomsticks in my time,' said Mrs Cantrip. 'I had one once – McShuttle it was called – made of the best Scottish heather. A beautiful, smooth movement it had.' Her eyes had a faraway look in them, and she went on in a singsong voice, 'From Pole to Pole we went once, in a single night, without so much as a jolt or jar, and obedient –'

'Oh, I know!' interrupted Miss Dibdin crossly. 'It singed its tail in the Northern Lights, and you never knew till you got home again. You've told me dozens of times. I'm sure I said all the things over my broom you told me to, when I bound the twigs on, and I used all the Flying Philtre there was. There's not a drop left. Now if only the rocking chair –'

'The rocking chair!' said Mrs Cantrip with withering scorn. 'Armchair flying! Soft, all you young witches nowadays! Do you think I'd be seen dead in it if I had not gone out of business? Not I! Now, when I was young –!'

'Ladies, ladies!' broke in the voice of Queen Grisana. It was a soft languid voice. 'Let us have no unpleasantness! There is nothing I dislike so much. Now let us have a cozy little chat together and I will tell you why I have summoned you.'

The voice seemed to have a slight purr behind it, but the green eyes flashed hard and brilliant from one to the other.

'It seemed to me that we might strike a bargain. I can be frank, because there is no danger of our being overheard. I have forbidden my people to use this high place tonight. It can be reached only by two paths which are closely guarded. My sentries will give instant warning if they see anything unusual. These children you mentioned, have you any reason to suspect that they know anything of our meeting?'

'The meddlesome brats are the only ones who could get here. They've stolen my Flying Chair. I'm uneasy in my bones. Reliable my bones is, as a rule,' said Mrs Cantrip.

'Then let us be quick in what we have to say,' purred the grey cat. She lowered her voice, so that the children had to lean forward to hear her. 'And what we say must never go further than this clump of trees. Now listen carefully!'

Mrs Cantrip and Miss Dibdin, their argument forgotten, craned forward. Grisana continued, 'My dear husband is getting old. A better king and husband you could never find, but he has no ambition. Ambition!' she repeated, lingering lovingly on the word. 'My son, my handsome Gracilis for whom this scheme is planned, is in many ways like his dear father – he must hear no whisper of this – but I, I have enough ambition for the three of us.'

There was no purr behind her words now. Rosemary blinked. It was hard to believe that the steely voice they heard belonged to the same animal.

'Fallowhithe and Broomhurst in a few days will be as one town,' she rapped out. 'One town, one King! And that shall not be Carbonel but Castrum, and I, I shall be Queen!'

She threw back her head, and a strangely triumphant, wailing cry rose on the night air, and sank again to a throaty murmur.

'For your dear son's sake, of course!' said Mrs Cantrip dryly.

'For my dear son's sake!' repeated Grisana, and once more her voice was soft and purring.

'Well, I'm with you on anything that means trouble for Carbonel. We're old enemies!' said Mrs Cantrip. 'I hate him!'

'I rather thought you did!' said the grey cat sweetly.

The old woman rubbed the side of her nose with a bony finger.

'What do you want us to do?'

'Just this,' went on Grisana. 'If, on the day that the last wall of the last house goes up between the two towns, you could see to it that Queen Blandamour – disappears – no violence of course – there will be such confusion in Fallowhithe that, when my armies pour into the town, they will meet with little or no resistance. No bloodshed, and a minimum of unpleasantness. I do so dislike unpleasantness.'

'It's lucky for you that the Kings are out of the way answering the Summons. If you succeed, what will your husband do when he returns?'

'What I tell him!' purred Grisana very sweetly. 'I told you he was growing old!'

'And Carbonel's kittens? I hear there are two of 'em,' said Mrs Cantrip. 'They might prove a rallying point for the Fallowhithe cats even without Blandamour.'

'True,' said Grisana. 'Perhaps they too had better ... disappear! The sooner the better. That will spread a little alarm in advance. Most useful. The dear little things!'

John could hear Rosemary breathing hard with indignation, and he put out a restraining hand.

Mrs Cantrip chuckled. It was not a nice noise. She clapped her hands on her bony knees. 'It's as nice a bit of mischief as I've come across in a week of wet Wednesdays. In plain English, you want the three of them kidnapped? All right. We'll do it!' said Mrs Cantrip.

'That's all very well, but what do I get out of it?' said Miss Dibdin huffily. 'I haven't been consulted!'

'Ah, but just think, dear!' the old woman wheedled. 'You'll maybe put all you've learned into practice! What a chance! Poor old Mother Cantrip can do no more magic now!'

'And you shall have your pick of all the kittens in the two towns to bring up as your cat!' said Queen Grisana.

'That's generous, dear! Don't turn it down. I always say a good cat can make or mar a young witch's magic.'

'Very well,' said Miss Dibdin grudgingly. 'I'll help. But I think you might have consulted me a little sooner.'

'Then that's settled,' said Mrs Cantrip. 'Well, we'd better be off.'

'I do hope the broom will behave better on the return journey,' said Miss Dibdin, licking her lips nervously.

'Better launch from the edge of the roof. It'll be easier,' said the old woman.

'I must go, too,' said Grisana. 'My son will be curious if I stay longer, and that would never do. What we parents must put up with for the sake of our children!' she purred affectedly.

John and Rosemary crouched among the vines. The crushed leaves smelt evilly, but they dared not lift their heads to watch, so what happened next they could only hear. There was a pause during which they imagined that Her Royal Greyness and her attendants must have gone their silent way.

Then they heard Mrs Cantrip say, 'She's gone. As wicked a piece of cat flesh as I've had the pleasure of meeting. Very satisfactory. "All for my dear son's sake!"' she mimicked. Then, in reply to a remark from Miss Dibdin which they did not hear, she added, 'Not likely! It's your broom, you can lead it!'

They heard the receding sound of a stick swishing through the grass. Cautiously they looked up. Miss Dibdin was leading the broom which alternately whipped around and lagged behind, like an unwilling dog on a leash.

'Better duck,' whispered John, 'in case the broom should circle above us when it's launched.'

They crouched in the grass once more.

There was a distant exclamation and a low laugh from Mrs Cantrip, and after a few moments' pause there was a whirr above them.

'They're off!' said John. 'That's funny, I thought I heard two things whizzing by!'

'So did I!' said Rosemary.

Both children sat up and gazed into the sky. Lurching down the wind was Miss Dibdin, clinging to the bucking broom for dear life. But beside her, travelling smoothly and easily, flew something else.

'The rocking chair! Quick!' said John. Together they dashed up the grassy slope over which they had crept with such caution. They scrambled up the little tree-crowned hill and peered anxiously over the other side.

'It's gone!' said John. 'They've taken the rocking chair!'

There was a dreadful pause. Then Rosemary said in a very small voice, 'How are we going to get home?'

13

Stranded

'How are we going to get home? My good girl, I don't know any more than you do!' said John, and because he was a little scared, he sounded cross. Then he was sorry. He thumped Rosemary on the back. 'Here, borrow my hankie,' he said, and untied it from his grazed knee.

Rosemary sniffed hard, looked at the handkerchief, shook her head and wiped her cheeks on the back of her hand.

'I'm all right now,' she said jerkily. 'We'd better explore. Perhaps we shall find a way down.'

'What about the two paths Grisana talked about?' said John. 'She said they were the only ways up here. Why don't you go round that side, and I'll go round the other.'

'No fear!' said Rosemary, 'I'm coming with you!'

The moon, round and full, still sailed across a cloudless sky. It shone on the grassy plateau of the high place, touching each leafy branch and every blade of grass with silver. Though it was almost as light as day, the shadows were very dark. Presently Rosemary said, 'I almost wish we could find Noggin or Swabber.' But there was no sign of life anywhere.

They walked around the edge of the high place together. Beyond was a sheer drop. 'What's that?' said John. 'Down there! Don't go too near the edge. Lie down and look over.'

They lay on their stomachs and peered over the edge.

Six feet down there was a narrow ledge which might be a path. They could see it winding its way down.

'Well, a cat could jump onto it with safety, but not a human,' said John, 'so that's no good. Let's find the other one.'

The second mountain path was no better. It wound steeply away down what looked like a sheer wall of chalk. Rosemary turned away from the dizzying view. She could see what looked like cats moving busily about their affairs on the hills clustered below them.

'I don't think there is anything we can do except wait until daylight,' she said.

They wandered back toward the tree-crowned hill where they had first landed. As they came to the little stream, Rosemary said, 'It doesn't look like water. It's white! Do you think it could possibly be milk? I'm awfully thirsty!'

She knelt down, drank a little from her cupped hands, but I'm sorry to say she spat it out again.

'What's it like?' asked John.

'It's milk all right, but it tastes like milk that's had haddock boiled in it! Let's sit down.'

She suddenly felt very, very tired, and they sat down with their backs against a tree trunk.

'Mrs Cantrip said she would have to find out where the kittens are,' she said sleepily. 'I expect it will take her some time, but we ought to make some sort of plan.'

'All right,' said John, and he yawned. 'Let's think.' But like Swabber, they both 'thought' with their eyes closed and in five minutes they were fast asleep.

It was John who woke first.

'Rosie! Wake up! It's morning!' he said.

Rosemary sat up, rubbed the sleep from her eyes

and looked around. No longer were they sitting on a grassy bank, but on a hard, zinc-covered roof, their backs against a ventilator shaft. It was a grey morning with a chill little breeze that found its way through Rosemary's dressing gown. She shivered. John turned up the collar of his jacket. They looked about them, at the grey expanse of roof. Where the stream had chuckled along its weed-fringed way was a gutter; where the thicket of trees had stood was a group of television aerials.

'Let's have a look at the mountain paths!' said John. 'Perhaps they've turned into something useful.'

They ran to the edge of the roof. The 'mountain paths' had certainly turned into something useful for the occupiers of all the ten floors of offices below, but not to anyone unlucky enough to be stranded on the roof. The two fire escapes they had become stopped short at the top floor. Neither of the escapes went up as high as the roof itself.

'If only we had a rope! We could let ourselves down,' said John. 'We might try tearing your nightdress into strips.'

'We certainly might not!' said Rosemary. 'If you think I'm going home in nothing but a dressing gown —' She stopped as a distant clock struck, and caught John's arm. 'We *must* get home somehow, it's seven o'clock! Mother will be worried stiff if she finds we aren't there, and we promised not to be inconsiderate. What shall we do?'

'There simply must be some way up onto the roof,' said John desperately. 'What's that triangular thing sticking up over there?'

They ran to look. In the side of a triangular erection, facing away from where they had been standing, was a door. They rattled the handle, but it was locked.

They did not stop to argue. They hammered on it with their fists and shouted for all they were worth, and after what seemed an age, it opened outwards suddenly. They were nearly knocked off their feet. Just inside, at the top of a flight of stairs, stood a very fat woman in a sacking apron, holding a broom with both hands above her head, as if ready to defend herself against all comers. When she saw John and Rosemary, she lowered the broom.

'Well, I don't know! A couple of children! Are there any more of you?' she asked suspiciously, peering around the door.

'Only us two, John and Rosemary.'

'You were making enough noise for twenty,' said the old woman. 'I'd just started scrubbing them top stairs when I heard a shouting and banging like the Day of Judgement. "Burglars!" I said to myself. "I'm off." And then I said, "Sounds like kids' voices. It's them boys again, I'll be bound. I'll get even with 'em!" So up I comes. But whatever next! What are you doing up here?'

'Oh, please!' said Rosemary. 'Please let us out. We must get home! Mummy will be so worried. They left us and we couldn't get down!'

'Locked you up there? You poor little things. You ought to be ashamed of getting your little sister into trouble like this!' the old woman said to John.

John opened his mouth to protest, but thought better of it, and she went on, 'Well, you'd better come down, the pair of you.'

She took Rosemary by the hand, not unkindly. 'Why, you feel starved with cold, love! I've got a kettle on downstairs for a cup of cocoa. You'd better have a drop to warm you up. You'll have to walk down – the lift don't work till nine.'

She shut the door and shot the bolts home. Thankfully, the children followed her. There were ten floors to pass. She went down in front of them, telling them over her shoulder that she was getting her work done early because her son had been 'took bad', and she wanted to get home to him, and about the battle she waged against dirty footmarks on the stairs, and boys in general, and that she could not understand how in the world they could have got up to the roof. John made a halfhearted attempt to defend 'them boys' After all, they were not to blame this time, but the old woman swept his explanation on one side with an indignant 'Don't you tell me!'

At last she led them down to a little room in the basement. Here they found a sink, a metal cupboard, a chair and a table. On the table stood an electric kettle which was already blowing steam through its spout like an angry dragon. She got a mug and two cups from the cupboard, a tin of cocoa and another of condensed milk, and in each mug she made a rich, dark brew. It was not cocoa as they knew it, but it was sweet and comforting, and put new courage into them. They drank while sitting on two upturned buckets.

'Lucky for you I was early,' the old woman said, between gulps of scalding cocoa. 'Now then, suppose you tell me all about it!' Her eyes were shrewd over the rim of the mug.

'Well,' said John slowly. 'We can't tell you *all* about it, because of the others. But we got onto the roof when they were there, and then ... well, they left us up there, on purpose I think, and we couldn't get down.'

'Well, I must say, I like a lad who won't tell on his pals, but you can tell them from me that next time I catch hair or hide of 'em lurking on my roof, there'll be real trouble. You're a nicely spoken pair of little things, I'll say that, but let this be a lesson to you. Steer clear of them boys! And if ever I find you up there again —' She blew noisily on the hot cocoa and left them to imagine the awfulness of the punishment that would be in store.

'Then you won't say anything to anyone this time?' said Rosemary. 'You are a darling! We'll never do it again, and we shall never forget how kind you've been!'

The old woman's eyes twinkled. 'Well, I like a bit of fun myself. Always did! And believe it or not, I was young once myself. Where do you live?'

'Fallowhithe,' said Rosemary.

'Fallow ... ?'

The old woman put down her mug with such a bump that the cocoa slopped over. She stared at Rosemary.

' 'Ere, don't tell me you're in your night things?'

Rosemary nodded.

'You been up there all night?'

Rosemary nodded again.

'Your poor ma will be frantic! Have you got your bus fares home? You haven't? Well, I don't know! 'Ere you are.' She took a worn black purse from her pocket and pushed a shilling into John's hand. When they tried to thank her she seemed embarrassed.

'All right, all right, you can send it back, dear. Flackett's the name, Number 1 Adelaide Row. Now hop it, or I shan't get my work done early after all.'

John and Rosemary did not have to be told twice. But before finally going out into the street, Rosemary tied up her nightdress with her dressing gown cord.

'It's a good thing your dressing gown has got too small,' said John. 'It looks like a coat.'

'I hope everyone else will think so,' said Rosemary doubtfully.

But people who travel on buses between seven and eight in the morning do not bother very much about what their fellow travellers are wearing. Apart from a wink and a 'What's this, the babes in the wood?' from the conductor, for there were no other children, they reached the end of Cranshaw Road without any more adventures.

As they turned into number 101, John said, 'We never made any plans last night after all about keeping the kittens safe. Let's look in before we go up to breakfast and tell Woppit to be specially careful.'

Rosemary nodded.

'And we must get those screws for the lock straight away,' she said as they ran across the lawn. They could see the greenhouse from the bottom of the path.

'Oh!' she said. 'The door's open! Come on!'

Together they raced down the path and looked inside. The flower pots they had stacked in one corner so neatly were upset and were scattered over the floor. The basket, in which the kittens slept, was on its side. The blanket was not there.

'Calidor! Pergamond!' called Rosemary sharply.

There was no reply. Only a plaintive squeak from the swinging door broke the silence. Frantically, they searched in every corner, they parted the strands of the creeper that grew up the sides of the greenhouse, they turned the watering can upside down, they even peered through the grating in the floor and as they searched they called. But there was no sign of the kittens.

'It's no use,' said Rosemary. 'They've gone!'

14

Gone!

JOHN and Rosemary stood and looked at each other in horrified silence. And then the silence was broken.

'What's that?' said Rosemary sharply. 'Listen!' It was a strangled 'mew!' which seemed to come from somewhere outside the greenhouse. The two children ran through the open door and looked around anxiously. Propped against the wall was a large, cracked, earthenware pot, the kind that gardeners sometimes use for forcing rhubarb. The hole at the top was covered with a brick, but it was from underneath that the sounds came.

'Quick!' said John. The mews were growing stronger.

They lifted the pot, but it was not the kittens they could hear. It was Woppit. The old cat was trying to free herself from the folds of the kittens' blanket in which she had been rolled.

'Woppit, dear!' said Rosemary, as she unwound the struggling animal. 'The kittens have gone! What has happened?' But Woppit was too ruffled and woebegone to explain.

'My little, kingly kittens!' she wailed. 'My furry darlings! They've gone! They've taken them away, and old Woppit still alive to tell! The shame of it!'

She rocked herself, moaning, from side to side. Rosemary lifted the rumpled animal onto her lap, but Woppit refused to be comforted.

'I'm quite sure you did everything you could!' said Rosemary, 'but tell us what happened!'

'They were sleeping in their bed,' said Woppit, 'so sweet and snug as two little sardines in a tin, and the moon was shining down on them so round and white as a bowl of milk, and there was me standing guard, and humming a little song and never dreaming –' She broke off, lifted her untidy whiskers to the sky and wailed again.

'Oh, do go on, Woppit!' said John. 'If only you'd tell us what happened, perhaps we could *do* something!'

'Peaceful as a kitchen hearthrug it was,' she continued. 'And then suddenly the door opened, and there was them humans!'

'What were they like?' asked Rosemary.

'There was a tall thin one with Persian fur that needed a deal of licking, and a short sleek one.'

'Persian fur?' repeated John.

'I guessed as much,' said Rosemary. 'It must have been Mrs Cantrip. Her hair sticks out around her face when it's untidy, rather like a Persian cat, and "sleek" is a very good description of Miss Dibdin. But how did they find out the kittens were here?'

'Search me!' said John shortly.

'Go on, Woppit. What did they do?'

'Do?' went on Woppit, rocking herself from side to side in her distress. 'They stood over the basket, and

Persian stirs my precious pets with her great bony finger and says, "We're in luck, my dear! It's them sure enough. It's Carbonel's kittens!"

'And Sleek says, "How do you know, dear?"

' "By the three white hairs at the tips of their little tails. The sign of all royal cats and kittens. Didn't they teach you anything at Oxford?"

'And Sleek claps her hands and says, "What a stroke of luck!" and she laughs, as pleased as if she'd found a couple of kipper heads in a bowl of cream. "Let's take 'em and go!" she says, and she bends down to scoop up my little furry loves.

' "Not without reckoning with me!" I says, and I ups and claws her hand good and proper. Well, she lets out a screech so loud as if she'd got her tail caught in the door. But Persian tumbles my darlings on to the floor, whips the blanket out of the basket and drops it on top of me. Mind you, I got in a left and right that'll leave a mark for a bit, but it weren't no good. She rolls me up and puts me in that dark place, and then she cackles through the hole at the top, "You can tell them children they may be clever, but Katie Cantrip has still got a trick up her sleeve! I might have known they'd get themselves mixed up in this!" And then she claps something on top of the pot so that I can't even hear what happens to my little purring, furry sweetings!'

The old cat lifted her muzzle and wailed again.

'Look, Woppit, dear. You don't have to tell us how frightful it is. We know. But we must go back to the flat now. We'll come back as soon as we can after breakfast.'

'We've simply got to keep our heads,' said John.

'The best thing you can do is to wait here until

Blandamour comes, and tell her what's happened,' Rosemary added.

'We've had some excitement, too, I can tell you!' said John.

The two children ran toward the house. When they reached the path from which they had set out the night before, Rosemary stopped.

'Look at that, John!'

'What, those two great skid marks on the gravel?'

'Yes, don't you see what it means?'

'Well, I suppose it means that we've got to get the garden roller and roll it flat again,' said John crossly. 'It must have been the weight of the two of us in the chair last night. Oh, come on, Rosie. I could eat a huge breakfast. Hope it's fried eggs.'

'But it wasn't us!' persisted Rosemary. 'Those are the marks of the rocking chair coming back with Mrs Cantrip! I think it did the same to her as it did to me. Of course it's a dear, but I don't think it's very bright. When you tell it to go home, it simply goes back to wherever it started from. It doesn't stop to think which house belongs to which person.'

John whistled, fried eggs forgotten for the moment.

'So when Mrs Cantrip told it to take her home, it brought her to your house by mistake, and I expect the broom with Miss Dibdin followed.'

Rosemary nodded.

'And I suppose the two of them thought they'd look around while they were here, so that's how they found the kittens. Almost by mistake! What rotten luck!'

'We've got to think of some way out of this as we've never thought before,' said Rosemary.

'Well, it's no use trying to think on empty stomachs. Do come on!'

Rosemary hurried, and together they burst into the apartment. The adventures of the night before had paled before this new anxiety. They rushed into the kitchen where Mrs Brown was frying eggs and bacon.

'Mother! The kittens have gone!' said Rosemary. 'They aren't anywhere to be found. Whatever shall we do?'

Her mother lifted a fried egg and slid it carefully onto a piece of fried bread. Then she looked up, and said with maddening grown-up detachment, 'Do, darling? Well, first of all you had better get dressed and then both of you must have a thorough wash! Where have you been? I don't mind you getting up early, but Rosie, I think you're a bit big to go wandering about the garden in your night things.'

'Yes, Mummy, but the kittens –!'

Her mother smiled. 'I expect they're somewhere in the garden, darling. Don't worry. Run off and dress now.'

Rosemary ran.

*   *   *

As soon as they were able after breakfast, which, for John at least, was a thorough-going affair of cereal, bacon and egg, and toast and marmalade, the children escaped to the garden. As they went into the greenhouse, Blandamour ran to meet them. Merbeck sat in respectful attendance in the background, and Woppit lay on the floor with her front paws over her nose moaning quietly to herself.

'Has she told you what's happened?' asked Rosemary.

'She has told me, poor, faithful creature,' said Blandamour. 'My unhappy little ones!'

'It is a bad business, your Majesty,' said Merbeck. 'It could not be much worse!'

'Oh, couldn't it?' said John. 'You haven't heard half of it yet. You see, last night –!'

He began the story of their adventure, and then Rosemary broke in and finished the tale. And as they recounted Grisana's wicked plot, Woppit stopped moaning and sat up to listen, and Blandamour fixed them with unwavering blue eyes, motionless except for the angry twitching of her long white tail.

'Then Grisana thinks that with me and my kittens out of the way, she and her Broomhurst crowd will be able to walk into my country and take possession, without a claw being raised in its defence! She is so unused to a well-governed kingdom that she mistakes the contentment of Fallowhithe cats for lack of spirit! And I, Blandamour, am to disappear! She talks as if I were a kitten with its eyes closed. I assure you I can defend myself!'

The white cat was pacing up and down now with flattened ears and bristling back.

'There will be many to defend you, your Majesty, should it come to that. But the first part of Grisana's plan has succeeded,' said Merbeck. 'The royal kittens have gone.'

'My poor little children. What will become of them?'

'Your Majesty!' said John suddenly.

All through Rosemary's account of their adventures, he had been busy digging out a loose tile from the floor with the toe of his shoe. His face was very red, 'Your Majesty, it's my fault, about the kittens I mean. If I had finished mending the lock, as I meant to last night, it would never have happened.'

'It's just as much my fault,' said Rosemary loyally.

'Somehow or other, we'll find the kittens and bring them back safely,' went on John. 'Won't we, Rosie?'

Rosemary nodded.

Blandamour looked searchingly at them both.

'If anyone can, I think you will. When the Kings return, my dear husband will thank you as you deserve for all you have done for us. When that day comes, all will be well again. Until then, we must keep this grasping Grisana at bay!'

'Your Majesty,' said Merbeck, stepping forward. 'I am old, my claws are blunt and my flanks are lean, but my blood races like a young animal at the tale of such wickedness! If your subjects know of this foul plot too soon, there will be bloodshed. And that we must avoid. Hot-headed young animals would bandy words with Broomhurst cats, and that would lead to blows. There would be border incidents, sallies into enemy country and eventually open war. I have seen it happen before.'

'Then what shall we do?' asked Blandamour.

'For the moment the hardest thing of all. Nothing,' said Merbeck. 'Only a few trusted animals must know of this plot until the time is ripe!'

'But my poor stolen kittens!'

'They can only be recovered by cunning, not force,' said Merbeck.

'But they are going to try to kidnap Queen Blandamour as well!' said Rosemary.

'Not until the day of the attack!' said Merbeck. 'And that will not be until the night of the day the last house is finished.'

'You are right, Merbeck,' said Blandamour. 'When my dear husband returns he must find every cat in his kingdom unharmed! I shall go about my usual business until the day the last house is built.'

'But —'

'Thanks to you, my faithful John and Rosemary, we shall be ready for them. Woppit will stay here and act as your messenger. I shall keep in close touch with you, and if my spies hear any news of my precious kittens —' her voice broke but she pulled herself bravely together — 'you shall hear at once!'

'Come on, Rosie,' said John. 'We must find Mrs Cantrip, and see if we can get her to let anything out!'

'I suppose we must,' said Rosemary reluctantly.

15

Miss Dibdin's Magic

WHEN John knocked at Mrs Cantrip's door, there was no answer. But knowing that this did not necessarily mean she was not at home, he went on knocking, quite politely but firmly. Presently they heard footsteps on the other side of the door, not Mrs Cantrip's shuffling tread, but the sharp click of high heels in a hurry. The door opened, and there was Miss Dibdin. She was wearing a large, embroidered apron, and her face was rather red. She held a wooden spoon in one hand.

'Oh, it's you, is it?' she said ungraciously. 'I thought it was the postman, or I should never have come down. What do you want?'

'We want to speak to Mrs Cantrip, please,' said John.

'She's out, and I can't stop talking here. I've got a most important piece of magic on the simmer. Go away.'

'Oh, but please –' began Rosemary.

'There now, it's boiling over. I'm sure I can smell it! You'd better come inside.'

A strange, sharp smell reached the children's noses, and as Miss Dibdin closed the door behind them, it became almost overpowering. She led them at a run, not into the kitchen, but up a flight of dark, steep stairs, into a room they had never seen before.

It was clearly a bed-sitting room. There was a bed in one corner, a wicker chair, a wardrobe and a table. The bed was made of tarnished brass, and two of its knobs were missing. A piece of folded cardboard shored up one of the table legs. There was a very old-fashioned gas fire in which the flames flickered in a blue and rather chilly way among the broken burners. Sprouting from the side of the fireplace was a gas ring. Propped up on the mantelpiece above, was a large, open book.

Miss Dibdin rushed forward and fell on her knees on the shabby rag rug which lay in front of the hearth.

'It worked!' she cried excitedly. 'I've done it!'

'Done what?' asked John.

'Look at the saucepan!' she said dramatically. The children looked where she was pointing.

'But there isn't a saucepan!' said Rosemary.

'That's just the point!' said Miss Dibdin excitedly. 'I've made it invisible!'

The children stared at the fireplace. The gas ring was lit. They could see the blue flames radiating like the petals of some strange blue flower, but they could see no saucepan, only what looked at first like a pale green jelly, apparently suspended just above the ring.

But it was not a jelly. It was a liquid, which was steaming and bubbling as merrily as water before an egg is put in to boil.

Miss Dibdin plunged her wooden spoon in the liquid. There was a little hiss, and at once the spoon disappeared, though John and Rosemary could see from the vigorous twisting of her wrist that she was stirring the bubbling mixture. Miss Dibdin cooed with delight.

'Good Heavens!' said Rosemary.

With little squeals of pleasure, Miss Dibdin began darting round the room carrying the invisible saucepan. The children could see the green liquid suspended in mid-air, about a foot away from the hand which seemed to be grasping the handle. With the invisible spoon, Miss Dibdin dropped a small blob of the mixture on the kitchen scales which stood on the table.

There was a tiny hiss and the scales disappeared. Next she tried a bunch of herbs that lay beside it. That disappeared, too. A brown paper bag, a saucer with something pink and rather horrid looking in it, all the things she had used to make her magic, disappeared one after another as she touched them with the dripping spoon. Her brush and comb on the rickety dressing table, the candlestick by her bed, one of the bedroom slippers by the chair, they all snuffed out as completely as the flame of a candle on a birthday cake.

'How absolutely smashing!' said John. 'You are clever!'

Miss Dibdin flushed with pleasure. 'I really think that even Katie will have to admit that it is quite creditable! She is always so crushing about my little efforts, though I must admit I have never succeeded in getting a spell to work before!'

As she spoke she gave a playful tap to the basket chair, and it was gone!

'Won't it be a little awkward living in a room with invisible furniture?' asked Rosemary, as the brass bedstead disappeared, leaving the bedclothes, which had not been touched, still neatly tucked in and apparently floating on air.

'Perhaps it will, dear. What a practical little thing you are! Just one more – I can't resist it!' And she made a playful dab at the wardrobe. It disappeared, too, suddenly revealing a row of clothes inside hanging on a row of invisible pegs, with a neat line of shoes apparently floating beneath.

'You must admit, it's enough to go to anyone's head a little!' She laughed. 'Of course I should really have made the counter-spell first, to make things visible again, but I've got the recipe all ready here!'

She tapped with the wooden spoon on the large book which was propped up on the mantelpiece, quite forgetting for the moment its magic properties, and lo and behold! The book disappeared, too. This time she did not laugh. She gave a horrified gasp.

'Oh, whatever have I done? How can I brew a counter-spell from an invisible book? Oh, silly me!'

'Well, couldn't you find another book?' asked Rosemary.

'You don't understand,' moaned Miss Dibdin. 'No two spells are ever alike! You can't brew a spell from one book and a counter-spell from another. It wouldn't work!'

'Where did you get your book from?' asked John curiously.

Miss Dibdin put the saucepan back on the ring, felt for the invisible chair, and sank despondently into it. The result looked very odd indeed.

'I found it in the library,' she went on. 'That was really what started it all. You must have noticed that most reference library users are rather elderly, and find stooping a little difficult? Well, I don't believe the books on the bottom shelves of the Fallowhithe Library ever get looked at at all, and it was there I found this one, in a dark corner, covered with dust and cobwebs. I thought it would make such an interesting hobby for the summer holidays.'

'But I thought you couldn't take reference books home?' said John.

'Well, of course you can't, but the girl in charge that day was one of my old pupils, and I persuaded her to let me, just this once. Oh dear, what have I done?'

The invisible basketwork gave a protesting creak as Miss Dibdin heaved miserably in the chair. 'Think of the fine I shall have to pay the library! And whatever will Katie say to the disappearance of all her furniture?'

She jumped up and felt anxiously along the mantelpiece to reassure herself that the book was still there. But it is difficult to pick up a large invisible book which is propped insecurely on a narrow shelf. There was a slithering sound, as the book was dislodged by her fumbling fingers, and it slipped off the mantelpiece. It hit the saucepan handle with such force that the pan overturned, and the liquid slopped on to the hearth. The rag rug promptly disappeared. What sort of noise the book made when it fell on to the hearth rug nobody noticed, because of Miss Dibdin's loud cry of distress.

'It's all upset. Oh, how clumsy of me! All that lovely vanishing mixture! And after so much trouble!'

'And what a mess!' said John. 'It's all over me. Lend me a hankie, Rosie!'

Rosemary turned and held out her handkerchief. But John was nowhere to be seen. The handkerchief was taken from her limp fingers by his invisible hand, and she watched fascinated, while it seemed to float unaided in the direction of his voice. When it reached the place where his waist would have been, the handkerchief, too, disappeared.

'John, don't! Oh, do come back!' said Rosemary in distress.

'Come back? What on earth do you mean?' said John.

Rosemary swallowed hard.

'You've gone invisible, too!'

16

Invisible

'Don't be so silly!' said John crossly.

'It's not silly, you are invisible!' said Rosemary, and she put out her hand to see if she could feel him. To her relief she could. He felt reassuringly warm and solid.

'Well, you needn't put your finger in my eye!' he said.

'Oh, my dears, how exciting!' said Miss Dibdin, her depression forgotten. 'An invisible boy! Who would have thought I could do it!'

'Well, I jolly well wish you hadn't!' said John. 'What on earth is going to happen to me now?'

'It's a pity I can't make the counter-spell, of course,' said Miss Dibdin, 'but I expect you'll soon get accustomed to it, dear. It may even have its uses, you know!'

'I don't want to get accustomed to it,' said John, sulkily, and then he went on in quite a different voice, 'But pr'aps you're right! I may find it quite useful!' His voice came from somewhere near the hearth rug, as though he was stooping to pick something up.

'Now then,' he went on. 'Suppose you tell us where the royal kittens are hidden!'

This time his voice came, unexpectedly, a few inches from Miss Dibdin's ear, and she started uncomfortably.

'They aren't hidden,' she said, 'and although I'm grateful to you for taking such an active part in my little experiment, it's as much as my life is worth to tell you where the kittens are. Personally I'm thankful to be rid of them.' She rubbed her scratched hands tenderly as she spoke.

'Well, if you don't tell us,' said John, 'I might have to make you invisible, too. There is just about enough of the mixture left at the bottom of the saucepan!'

Rosemary turned to where a paper-thin pale-green disc lay on the hearth rug. She supposed this was all that was left at the bottom of the invisible saucepan. Fascinated, she watched it rise from the floor and heard John's voice keeping pace with it as it advanced towards the retreating figure of Miss Dibdin. The liquid frothed and winked in a hundred bubbles as John twirled the invisible pan. Miss Dibdin had her back against the wall now, and above her head the mixture had taken the shape of something that is just about to be poured.

'No!' she said, putting up her hands to ward it off. 'No! No! I don't want to be invisible.'

'I expect you'd get accustomed to it!' said John. 'And it may even have its uses! That's what you said to me, you know. But I won't do it if you tell me what you've done with the kittens!'

'All right! All right! I'll tell all I know, if you'll only put the saucepan down!'

Almost as anxiously as Miss Dibdin, Rosemary watched the green liquid right itself to a disc again and sink slowly onto the table. Miss Dibdin tottered across the room and sat heavily on the bed whose broken, but invisible springs jangled in protest.

'I'll tell you all I know, but it's not very much,' she said. 'Katie went off to sell them both this afternoon, somewhere in Broomhurst, because she said no one was likely to look for them there, and she might as well make a bit of money out of them. When I asked her where she was taking them she just laughed and said something about two pins in a packet, and two peas in a peck. That's all I know about it,' she ended sulkily.

'Thank you!' said John. 'Come on, Rosie.'

The handle of the door seemed to turn of its own accord, and the door itself swung open. Wide-eyed, Rosemary squeezed through as much as possible to one side. The door closed behind them.

'You needn't behave as though I've got the plague!' said John as they went down the uneven stairs. 'Being invisible may have its uses, but it's beastly unpleasant.'

'Oh, John, I'm so sorry!' Rosemary felt for his hand, and in the dimness of the little downstairs room she threw her arms around him and gave him a hug, a thing that ordinarily she would not have dreamed of doing.

'All right! All right!' said John uncomfortably. 'You needn't choke me!' But he said it in a voice that sounded comforted. 'Come on, you old Rosie!'

They opened the front door and went out into the sunlit street.

'Let's get home as quickly as possible,' said Rosemary to the sound of John's feet padding beside her. 'I'm glad you didn't do it, you know. I mean, I don't like Miss Dibdin much when you can see her, but invisible –! You don't think she'll start brewing any more from that book of hers, do you?'

'She won't!' said John cheerfully.

'But if she can make it uninvisible again?'

'It wouldn't help her much if she could, because she hasn't got it any longer. I picked it up from the hearth rug where it had fallen. But, of course, you couldn't either of you see it. And, my good girl, if you used your eyes you'd see that I've got the remains of the invisible mixture, too! She's done quite enough mischief with it already.'

Rosemary backed away nervously as the pale green circle floated towards her. 'Here, you'd better carry the saucepan. This book needs both hands,' said John. Rosemary felt gingerly for his arm and slid her fingers down onto the handle.

'But can you read it and find the counter-spell so that you can stop being invisible?' she persisted.

'Of course I can! Let's find somewhere quiet where we can sit down and I can have a look!'

'I'd much rather go home,' said Rosemary.

'I dare say, but you aren't invisible,' said John tartly.

A man in a bowler hat, carrying a brief case, bumped heavily into him and looked after them in a puzzled way.

'Oh, do come on!' said Rosemary. 'Poor man, it must be horrible to walk into an invisible boy.'

'And it's pretty horrible for an invisible boy to be walked into by a great hulking visible man. He trod on my foot, but I don't get any sympathy. Oh, no!'

Rosemary began hotly, 'Well anyway –' and then she stopped. 'Oh, don't let's squabble. If ever there was a time to stick together, it's now. Come on. Let's cross the road and go into the public gardens over there. We can sit on the steps of the statue.'

'If somebody thought they were going to sit on a seat and found themselves sitting on an invisible me, I should think they'd go potty,' said John gloomily.

Keeping close together they crossed the road. It was a small garden, bright with flower beds. In the centre was the statue of a departed benefactor of Fallowhithe. He stood forever leaning on a marble column. There were several mothers sitting on the wooden seats near by, knitting and gossiping in the sunshine, while their small children slept in prams or played around them.

'How silly marble trousers look!' said Rosemary.

'Never mind the statue!' said John, and pulled her down beside him on the top step. She put out her hand, and although she could not see it she felt the powdery leather of the book's ancient binding and the little breeze made by the paper as John hurriedly flicked the pages over.

'It's terribly difficult to read,' he said. 'The writing is all cramped and spidery. Now then, "Iniquity, invective,"' he read. 'Ah, here it is. "Invisibility".'

'Go on, read it!' said Rosemary, and John read out slowly. '"First take the pan, or pipkin formerly used for the Brew of Invisibility, and scour it thoroughly. Put in it seven eggshells full of water, so clear that it doth appear not to be there, and in the water place some transparent substance that by boiling will consume itself. Then by the light of a dwindled candle, seethe it until it shall have disappeared, stirring the meantime widdershins, and intoning this incantation ..."'

'Don't let's bother about the incantation now,' went on John. 'What does "widdershins" mean?'

'Widdershins means counterclockwise, like this,' said Rosemary, and she stirred an imaginary saucepan.

'I don't think it does,' said John. 'It means the other way.'

'No, this way!' said Rosemary impatiently.

'I bet it doesn't,' said John. 'And what does "intoning" mean?'

'It means singing, like this,' and she proceeded to show him. 'More or less li-i-i-ke this, like they do in chur-ur-urch!'

She stood up the better to show what stirring widder-shins meant and intoned, 'And anyway, I thi-i-i-ink we'd better go home to di-i-i-inner!'

She broke off as a soothing voice behind her said, 'Yes, dearie, I should. The very best thing you can do!'

She turned round. Looking up at her were three of the mothers.

'Poor little thing! Talking to herself and waving her arms about,' said one. 'I noticed her when she came in, and I thought then she looked a bit queer,' said another.

'I don't look queer!' said Rosemary indignantly.

'They ought not to let her out alone!' said a little old woman with a bulging shopping basket. 'They do say that talking to yourself is —'

'But I wasn't talking to myself,' Rosemary broke in.

'Then who were you talking to, dear?' said the first woman, in a voice that was meant to soothe, but only maddened Rosemary.

'Why, to John!' she said unwarily. 'He's sitting beside me on the steps here, only you can't see him, he's invisible. Oh, don't pull my skirt!' she went on, ignoring John's warning tweak, and pushing away the hand that no one could see.

A short fat woman nodded to her tall friend. 'I thought so, poor kid,' she said. 'I'll go and fetch a taxi, and you and Mrs Podbury see she doesn't come to any harm while I'm gone. Look after baby, Ida!' she called over her shoulder, and bustled off.

By this time a crowd of people had collected from nowhere, as crowds do, surrounding the steps and agreeing that it was a shame and that something ought to be done about it.

'Now you've done it!' said John under cover of the hum of discussion.

'Whatever shall we do?' said Rosemary desperately. Her face was red and her voice shook, but nothing would have made her give way to tears in front of so many people all oozing with unwanted sympathy.

'I don't know,' whispered John. 'But I'll stand by you!' and the hand he slipped into hers gave a heartening squeeze.

From their vantage point on the steps they could see over the heads of the crowd. A taxi had stopped just outside the entrance, and the short fat mother was hurrying towards them.

'Somehow we've got to create a diversion!' said John.

'Whatever's that?' asked Rosemary.

'You'll soon see!' answered John. 'Here, give me the saucepan!'

'For goodness' sake, don't make somebody else invisible!' said Rosemary in alarm.

'Not somebody, something!' said John from between tight lips. 'It's the only way!'

Mrs Podbury was advancing from the crowd.

'Now just tell me where you live, dear, and we'll take you home in a nice taxi!' she said in a cooing voice.

But Rosemary did not have to answer. With a twist of his wrist John tipped the remaining green liquid over the marble statue. There was a little hiss, and suddenly the steps were there, the pedestal was there, but the statue of Sir Bartle Boole, J.P., had vanished into thin air.

There was a moment's pause and then a gasp rose from the crowd, which wavered and fell back.

'I think it's time we went home to dinner!' said the

short fat mother faintly, and seizing her pram in one hand and the protesting Ida in the other, hurried away.

It suddenly seemed that no one in the crowd wanted to meet the eye of anyone else.

'Quick!' said John as the crowd began to melt. 'Now's our chance! Scram!'

Together they ran for the gate. Rosemary looked back once. The knot of people had disappeared as completely as the statue of Sir Bartle Boole, J.P. They dashed past the taxi, whose driver was looking angrily around for his fare, down the road and around the corner as fast as they could go.

'Let's go home!' panted John, 'before anything else happens! What a morning!'

17

Adelaide Row

WHEN they reached home, without a word John and Rosemary made for the Green Cave. Rosemary flopped down with a sigh of relief. She could see where John was sitting by the sudden flattening of grass and fallen leaves beside her. A couple of beetles scuttled away from his invisible weight, protesting in shrill, startled voices.

'I'm sorry we disturbed you!' said Rosemary.

'Nice manners! Nice manners!' chirruped a sparrow as it hopped onto the next bush.

'Now then,' said John. 'I've been doing some pretty hard thinking. We've got so many problems to solve that we shall just have to take them as they come. The first is, what are we to say to your mother about me? I can't go in to dinner like this!'

Rosemary frowned.

'Couldn't you send a note to say you've been called away on urgent business?' she suggested.

'Oh, be your age, Rosie!' said John. 'You know very well that your mother would want to know what the urgent business was. And if you told her, she wouldn't believe a word of it. I shouldn't blame her, either.'

'Well, supposing ... I know! Go to the telephone box at the end of the road, ring up the Williamses in the flat below, and ask if you can speak to Mum. All you need do is remind her that you were going to see your aunt one day, and would it matter if you did not come home for dinner, and then ring off quickly before she asks awkward questions. I've got tuppence.'

John had a penny, and two halfpennies which a kindly passer-by changed for them. Rosemary went with him to the call box. She watched the receiver apparently leap into the air and remain suspended, as John clamped it against his ear. She heard the pennies drop and saw the dial whizzing around of its own accord. After a pause the receiver floated down again and the door suddenly burst open, bumping her painfully on the nose.

'Sorry,' said John. 'I forgot you couldn't see I was coming out. It's all right. Your mother didn't seem to mind a bit. But you'd better hurry up because dinner has been ready for half an hour and it's spoiling. It's my favourite, steak and kidney pie and chocolate blancmange. Just my luck.'

'I'll bring you some to the greenhouse,' said Rosemary, 'as soon as I can. You'd better see if Woppit has had any message from Blandamour.'

It was rather an uncomfortable meal, spent in heading her mother off the subject of John's sudden passionate desire to see an aunt of whom he was not usually very fond. After dinner, Rosemary was just putting a generous helping on a plate for John when her mother said, 'Really, darling, I don't think we can feed Woppit on steak and kidney pie! I've put some fish scraps on the cracked dish in the meat safe for her. Wash the dishes for me, dear, will you? I've promised to go round to old Mrs Hobby to fit her for a new summer frock. You know she can't get out much now. I'm afraid you'll have to see to your own tea, darling. I hope you won't be lonely.'

'I shall be too busy looking for the kittens, Mummy. We simply must find them,' said Rosemary.

When she reached the greenhouse carrying the cracked dish, she found Woppit curled up asleep on John's knee. She was getting used to seeing the things that he was holding floating in the air. It seemed that the old cat had accepted his invisibility quite calmly. To her it was just another example of the unaccountable way that humans behave. She opened her eyes and jumped down at the word 'dinner', wriggling and writhing in a way that Rosemary found quite alarming until she realized that the cat was only rubbing herself against John's invisible ankles. She explained about the dinner.

'I'm afraid you and Woppit will have to share it.'

'If so be you can swallow into an invisible stomach,' said Woppit. 'You can have all mine and welcome. You've done your best for my little furry favourites, according to your lights. I'll say that for you.'

'It's very good of you,' said John hastily, putting the dish of congealed scraps onto the floor, 'but I wouldn't dream of taking any of it!'

'I managed to bring you some apples and biscuits,' said Rosemary.

'Well, that'll have to do,' said John in a resigned voice. 'Now look here, Rosie,' he went on between bites of apple, 'we can't do the counter-spell until to-night when the moon is up. Luckily it's on the wane. I've looked it up in my diary, so this afternoon let's concentrate on finding the kittens.'

There was a low moan from Woppit.

'Now all we know is that Mrs Cantrip sold them somewhere in Broomhurst this morning. Do shut up, Woppit. It's no use moaning. The only clue we've got is what she said to Miss Dibdin, "Two pins in a packet, two peas in a peck." Sounds nonsense to me.'

'Look here, John,' said Rosemary, 'there is one thing we must do first, and that is to pay back Mrs Flackett. It's a debt of honour.'

'I've been thinking that, too,' said John. 'I keep feeling I've heard the name Flackett before somewhere. Suppose we find out where Adelaide Row is and go there straight away.'

'And we can try to puzzle out what the "peas and pins" bit means as we go,' said Rosemary.

They found Adelaide Row in a street guide, and John put the remains of the five shillings his father had given him in his pocket, and Rosemary asked Mr Featherstone if she might pick a bunch of flowers to give to Mrs Flackett. By the time they had reached Broomhurst and actually found the house, it was growing late in the afternoon. They had talked of nothing else, but they were no nearer to guessing what Mrs Cantrip had meant by 'Two pins in a packet, two peas in a peck.'

Adelaide Row consisted of half a dozen houses so small that they might have been built for rather large dolls. At the back, the railway rushed and roared. The front gardens were overshadowed by the high blank wall of a warehouse, which was only the width of a narrow path away from the garden gates. But the houses had been freshly whitewashed, and most of the gardens, which were separated from one another by low green palings, managed to grow marigolds and nasturtiums and Virginia stock. In fact, they had the feeling of houses that had once been in the country and were surprised to find themselves in the middle of a town.

Mrs Flackett was sitting outside her front door on a kitchen chair, popping peas into a colander. Hanging from a hook in the little porch was a canary singing its head off.

'Yes, dearie?' said the old woman, as Rosemary walked up the path. 'What do you want? Why it's you, Rosemary, isn't it? Changed out of your nightie yet?'

Rosemary laughed and nodded.

'I've come to pay back the money you lent us. You were so awfully good to us, about the cocoa and not telling. We thought you might like a bunch of flowers. I was allowed to pick one of everything there was in the garden. The feathery stuff is parsley that's gone to seed. I think it's pretty.'

'Well!' said Mrs Flackett heartily. 'Isn't that kind of you, dear! There's nothing I like better than a bunch of flowers from a real garden. Shop ones is never the same somehow.'

The flowers were beginning to wilt, but she buried her round nose in them and gave a long sniff.

'I'll put 'em in a vase straight away. They'll soon perk up. Where's your friend John?'

'I'm meeting him ... presently,' said Rosemary truthfully. She had arranged to meet him by the garden gate on which, from its jerky way of opening and shutting, she guessed he must be swinging.

'Be a love and go on with them peas, will you? Just while I put the flowers in water.'

Mrs Flackett rose heavily to her feet and disappeared through the small front door. Rosemary knelt on the grass and went on popping the peas into the colander. It did not take her long to finish, and it is worth mentioning that she did not eat one.

'Two peas in a peck,' she said thoughtfully, plunging her hand into the colander and letting the peas trickle through her fingers.

'Peas in a peck! Peas in a peck!' sang the canary, up and down the scale like an opera singer. Rosemary looked up.

'There's some chickweed among the pea pods. Would you like it?' she said, standing on the chair and holding it up for the bird to see.

The canary stopped in mid trill, cocked its black eye and said, 'You just try me!'

'All right, here you are!' said Rosemary and pushed it through the bars of the cage.

'Very obliging of you, I'm sure,' said the bird, making little stabbing pecks at the chickweed. 'Quite common, hearing humans seem to be around here. But you aren't like the one inside. He claps his hands over his ears and groans every time I say anything to him. Bad manners, I call it!'

'Do you mean there is someone inside the house who understands you, too?' asked Rosemary.

But before the canary could answer, Mrs Flackett was back with a large slice of homemade currant cake on a willow pattern plate.

'Talking to my Joey, are you? He's a rascal, he is!' She looked up at the cage and whistled a tune and the bird whistled back.

'She isn't a hearing human,' he sang. 'But she as near understands what I say as makes no matter.'

'I've brought you a bit of cake,' went on Mrs Flackett. 'You must be hungry coming all that way, and here's a slice in a paper bag for your friend.'

'Thank you!' said Rosemary. 'I'm very hungry. May I eat it now?'

'I thought you didn't like boys,' she said presently. Mrs Flackett had lowered herself carefully into the chair.

'Not in the way of business, I don't,' she said. 'Messing up my nice clean stairs. Home's different, and there's boys and boys! Why bless me if you haven't finished the peas for me! I thought a nice chump chop and new potatoes with them might tempt my poor Albert for his tea.'

She sighed.

'Is he very ill?' asked Rosemary.

'Not to say ill in himself,' said Mrs Flackett. 'It's just that he . . . well, he imagines things.'

'What did I tell you?' sang the canary up and down the scale. Rosemary gave him a quick look. She knew better than to answer aloud.

'Stays in the house all day. He won't even go to work, and him doing so well! Always good at his books he was since he was a lad. He won't have the doctor; he won't even speak to his young lady. Ever so upset she is. She works in the same business, in the perfumery. Me being a widow, and him all I've got, I worry terrible.'

'But what does he imagine?' asked Rosemary, brushing the last of the cake crumbs off her lap.

'It all began when a black cat came into the shop, about a week ago. He says he distinctly heard it speak! Why you've dropped your plate, dearie!'

Rosemary picked it up, and her face was rather red.

'He doesn't work at Hedgem & Fudge, does he?' she asked faintly.

'Why, however did you guess?'

'I . . . I think I've heard the name before,' she answered lamely. 'I must go now and meet John.

Please, please don't worry about Albert! I'm sure he'll get well again!'

'I'm sure I hope so, dear,' said Mrs Flackett with a worried frown. Then she brightened. 'But come again any time you're passing!' she called as Rosemary went down the path.

'John! John! Where are you?' Rosemary whispered cautiously when she reached the gate.

'Here!' he said just by her ear. 'Where I said I'd be.'

'Oh, John, it's dreadful –!'

'I know, I know. I heard it all,' he said gloomily. 'I got bored watching you stuffing currant cake, and the canary stuffing chickweed. It's a funny thing, but wherever I look everyone is eating except me! Anyway, I came into the garden after a bit to see what was going on, and I heard. This magic is getting things in a mess!'

'Mrs Flackett sent a piece of cake for you,' said Rosemary, holding out the bag.

'Oh, good!' said John more cheerfully.

'All the same, I popped her peas for her and I've got an idea –'

'Come on!' said John. 'Let's find somewhere quiet where nobody will notice you talking to thin air, or me making currant cake disappear.'

18

Calidor

THEY turned the corner at the end of Adelaide Row and walked along the path that ran by the railway cutting. There was a wire fence on one side and a high wall on the other. Nobody was about, except two small boys with eyes for nothing but train spotting, so they sat down on a flight of steps which led up to the road.

'I'll tell you what I think,' said Rosemary. 'The pins in a packet and peas in a peck is quite simple really. I suddenly thought of it when I had finished popping Mrs Flackett's peas, and I saw them all in the colander. I think it just means that one pea is very like another, so that the best way to hide one special pea would be to put it with a peck of others. The same way with pins. One pin would be very hard to pick out in a packet.'

'Mm,' said John, in the fluffy voice of someone whose mouth is very full. 'That's very clever of you, Rosie! Well, the only place I can think of where there might be a whole lot of kittens is a pet shop.'

'I believe there's quite a big one in the new building in the market square. Mr Featherstone was telling me about it the other day. Come on! What are we waiting for?'

'Me, to finish my cake!' said John obstinately. 'It's all very well for you with steak and kidney pie inside you as well. I think that invisible insides need more food than other people's.'

'Your visible one seemed to think much the same thing,' said Rosemary.

'Oh well, if you imagine I'm just greedy,' said John, and trailed off into huffy silence. It was broken by the sound of voices behind them. Two cats were trotting down the steps.

'Well, I'll do my best, Fuggins,' said one of them, a sleek, rangy tabby. 'A lot of Broomhurst fellows have slipped in quietly already. The Fallowhithe animals don't seem to suspect. Simple creatures they are. Fish heads for us and tails for them when it's over, I think her Royal Greyness said?'

His huffiness forgotten, John whispered, 'Don't let on you understand!'

'And the pick of the best hearthrugs for Broomhurst animals!' said Fuggins. 'Only a few days to wait now, my boy! There's a gang of alley cats down here that I want to enroll. See you on . . . the night!'

Fuggins trotted purposefully away along the path, and the tabby, by means of a dustbin and a broken-down fence, leaped on to the wall and went along the top until he was out of sight.

'There were cats running along the warehouse wall all the time you were talking to Mrs Flackett,' said John. 'Dozens of them.'

'Don't you remember? Carbonel told us that wall tops are the main roads of Cat Country.'

'Things seem to be moving,' said John.

Rosemary guessed that he had got up because of the shower of crumbs which suddenly fell at her feet.

'Well, get on, girl!' he said impatiently.

'I like that!' said Rosemary hotly.

'That's a good thing,' said John maddeningly. 'This

way!' and Rosemary swallowed her crossness and hurried after the sound of his retreating footsteps.

The pet shop was not difficult to find. It was in the new block of shops next to Mrs Flackett's offices. They looked up as they passed. It was difficult by daylight to imagine its roof top was the same as the high place they had flown to with moon-flooded trees and milky stream. The shop they were looking for called itself 'Chez Poodles'.

'Oh, look! The whole of the window is full of kittens!' said Rosemary.

They stared through the window. On the floor, which was covered with shavings, were kittens sleeping, kittens fighting, kittens playing. There were drifts and heaps of kittens, black, grey, tabby and tortoiseshell. From the roof hung a mobile, and as it swung, they jumped and patted the bells and balls that hung from the moving arms, to the delight of the little knot of people in the street outside.

'But I can't see Pergamond or Calidor!' whispered John.

'Look over there!' said Rosemary.

Two kittens had begun a tussle in a corner, a black with white paws and a grey. It was not easy to distinguish them clearly as they rolled and tumbled, but there was something about the jaunty way in which the black one hurled himself on the grey which seemed familiar. By the time John was looking in the right direction, half a dozen more kittens had thrown themselves into the fight, and the black cat was hidden beneath a pile of thrusting noses and kicking legs.

'I'm sure it was Calidor!' said Rosemary.

As she spoke, the black kitten crawled out from the

bottom of the pile, and shaking each paw in turn, looked with interest at the mound of cats, still milling on top of one another.

'Go in and buy him, now!' said John, hurriedly pushing a handful of small change into Rosemary's hand. 'I'll wait outside.'

But as he spoke a white-overalled arm leaned over the wire barrier at the back of the window, and a hand picked up the black kitten by the scruff of his neck, and lifted him out of sight.

'Quick!' said John.

Rosemary dashed into the shop. By the window stood the assistant still holding Calidor by the scruff of his neck, while on the other hand she rested his hind legs through which curled his short tail.

'The three royal white hairs!' said Rosemary to herself. 'Calidor!' she said softly. 'It's me, Rosemary!'

The kitten gave a little soundless mew, and the two people who had been examining him, looked round. One was a small plump woman in a very fashionable but extremely unbecoming hat, and very high heels. The other was a girl of about Rosemary's age. But there the likeness ended, for she looked as though she had never been dirty in her life, and not one of the pale hairs of her ponytail was out of place. It must be admitted that one of Rosemary's plaits was in the knotted condition that results from pushing up the bow when it gets loose, instead of re-tying it, and there was a smudge on her cheek.

'Now do make up your mind, Dossy darling! First you want a grey kitten, and then a ginger, and now you want a black! Daddy said you could have one if you were good at the dentist's, and really you weren't very good so you shouldn't have one at all. But I do so hate to see her little face cloud over!' the woman went on to the assistant. But even with the prospect of a kitten that she did not deserve, Dossy's 'little face' seemed clouded. Rosemary thought she looked down-right cross.

'I want a white kitten!' announced Dossy.

'I'm afraid it just happens that we haven't one in the shop,' said the assistant with weary politeness. 'Not one.'

'Oh, please!' said Rosemary, who felt she could not wait a minute longer. 'May I have the black kitten? How much is it?'

But this was all that was needed to get Dossy to make up her mind.

'You can't have it!' she said. 'I'm buying it.'

'But you said you wanted a white one, and I must have it for a special reason!' said Rosemary desperately. 'It's a very special kitten!'

'Well then, if it's so very special, it's all the more rea-son why I should have it,' said Dossy tartly.

'I think my little girl must have first choice,' said the woman. 'We'll take the little black fellow after all!' She turned to the assistant and paid over the money.

'Please, may I hold him, just one minute?' said Rose-mary unhappily. She took the little animal in both hands and held him to her cheek. He felt very small beneath his fluff of coal black fur.

'You'll have to go with her,' she whispered.

'I don't want to, I don't like her!' said Calidor.

'We'll rescue you somehow. John is outside. You won't be able to see him because he is invisible. But I know he'll think of something.'

Calidor gave a sad little mew.

'Cheer up,' said Rosemary. 'Remember you are a royal kitten and you must be brave. Couldn't you manage a little purr? That's better! Where is Pergamond?'

'In a cage at the back of the shop by herself. I'm so glad to see you, Rosie!' he said. Calidor gave her cheek a little lick.

Dossy was looking on curiously.

'Mother!' she said in an aggrieved voice. 'That girl's talking to my kitten!'

'Take him to the car, darling, and show him to Daddy. I shan't be a minute.'

Rosemary handed Calidor over and followed Dossy's beautifully tailored but irritating back out of the shop.

'All right, I'm here!' whispered John's voice beside her.

'She's bought him!' said Rosemary. 'And now they're going off in a car and we don't know where to!'

'We'll soon find out!' said John.

'But how?'

'I'll go too! No one will see me! What a gorgeous car! I've always wanted to go in one of those high-powered things, and now's my chance!'

'I must stay here,' said Rosemary. 'Pergamond's at the back of the shop. Good luck, John!'

'Good luck, Rosie!'

The plump woman was getting into the front seat of the car. There was plenty of room for three. Rosemary saw the door at the back open and close noiselessly. She waved as the car slid smoothly into the traffic.

'Miss Dibdin was right. Being invisible has got its uses,' said Rosemary, and turned and went back into the pet shop.

19

The Pet Shop

AT any other time Rosemary felt she could have spent a long while quite happily looking around the shop. She went past the tanks of tropical fish which lined the side opposite the counter. Out of the corner of her eye she could see their jewelled shapes dart and hover in each small, watery world, but she walked resolutely by and pushed through the bead curtain which divided the shop from the animal cages. The noise here was deafening. It reminded her of Fairfax Market on Saturday night with all the stall-holders shouting their wares; only here each animal was trying to sell itself. Only the birds sang and gossiped to each other. It mattered little to them in what house their cages stood.

'Buy me! Buy me!' shouted a corgi puppy.

'Only ten shillings! Come along, come along!' called a pair of guinea pigs.

A case of hamsters squeaked, 'Buy! Buy! Buy!' and a large, buck rabbit wrinkled its nose in disdain at having to announce that it was going for fifteen and six.

A cockatoo whistled shrilly, 'All hands to the pump! How de do! How de do! How de do!' and rocked himself violently from side to side.

'Very well, thank you!' said Rosemary politely.

'Put a sock in it!' said the cockatoo rudely, and made clicking noises with its tongue.

Rosemary ignored him and searched the cages anxiously for Pergamond. She asked two Siamese cats if they had seen her. They stared insolently, and said something which she could not understand, presumably in Siamese. The few people who were looking at the animals as well, were unlikely to hear her whispered inquiries in the general hubbub.

Next she asked a tortoise. He looked up heavily from a lettuce leaf and said in a slow, deep voice, 'I don't know nothing about no kittens. But if it's tortoise-shell you want, why not have a tortoise in it? Have me!' And she realized by the curious jerking of its shell that the creature was laughing at what it thought was a joke. Rosemary shook her head.

'Pity,' said the tortoise, and went on eating lettuce.

She turned to a cage of white mice. But at the word 'kitten' there was a flick of tails and whiskers, and they all disappeared into a round hole in a wooden box at the back of the cage.

'Polly put the kettle on,' shrieked the cockatoo, and rattled its beak on the perch.

'A tortoise-shell kitten!' yapped a fox terrier puppy. 'Kittens? Yah! You want a puppy!' and he turned to bowl over his companion who had nipped him in the leg.

'But I keep telling you!' said Rosemary desperately. 'All I want is a kitten, and you won't listen!'

For a moment she was alone in the shop.

'Second from the left, top row!' said a voice. It was the cockatoo. He was standing motionless, his yellow crest thrust forward. Rosemary went up to his perch. When she first saw him she had thought he was rather like a clown at a circus. Now he looked suddenly very wise and very dignified.

'If I'd known you were a hearing human I should never have tried that "Polly-put-the-kettle-on" stuff on you. That's just in the way of business. I must give my public what it wants, you know. They put a tortoise-shell kitten up there in a cage by herself, because of her markings. Quite rare, apparently.'

'Oh, thank you!' said Rosemary gratefully and ran to look.

'Don't mention it!' said the cockatoo, and as an old lady with a small boy came in through the bead curtain he shrieked, 'All hands to the pump! How de do! How de do! How de do!' to the small boy's delight.

At the back of the second cage from the left, in the top row, was a small, furry, tortoise-shell ball.

'Pergamond! It's me, Rosemary! Do wake up, Pergamond!'

The kitten uncurled herself, and yawned so wide that Rosemary could see the little pink wrinkles on the roof of her mouth.

'What a long time you've been,' she said sleepily. 'But I knew you'd come!' and she got up and rubbed herself against the cage door. Rosemary stroked her with a single finger, which was all she could poke through.

'How much are you, Pergamond dear?'

'Six shillings,' she said proudly.

'Oh no!' said Rosemary in dismay. 'I've only got four and elevenpence and an Irish halfpenny!'

'Well, you can't expect me to go for tuppence,' said the kitten grandly. 'Not rare markings *and* royalty!'

'Ssh!' said Rosemary, looking around nervously. 'Don't let anyone know who you are!'

'Well, I don't see –' began Pergamond, and broke off as the corgi puppy next door hurled himself at the dividing wire netting, yapping defiance at all kittens.

Undaunted, Pergamond advanced on him, spitting and swearing.

'Pergamond!' said Rosemary in a shocked voice. 'What would Woppit say?'

'You can't expect anything else,' said the cockatoo. 'A very mixed lot here! They pick up all sorts of expressions. I suppose,' he went on, sidling toward her, 'as well as a kitten you wouldn't be wanting a cockatoo? Thirty pounds and cheap at the price.'

'Thirty pounds! Why I haven't even six shillings to buy my kitten. What can I do?'

'Oh well!' said the cockatoo, and sighed deeply. Then he went on, 'You might consult the boss, Bodkin is the name. Not a bad sort as a rule! But you're out of luck today, he's got toothache.'

Rosemary returned to the comparative quiet of the shop where a large man in a white overall was selling a guinea pig to a girl. She waited until the girl had gone and then she said, 'Excuse me, but what do your customers usually do when they find they haven't got quite enough money to buy something?'

'Go away until they can get it,' said Mr Bodkin shortly, and shut the drawer of the till with a snap.

Rosemary had to admit to herself that he was quite right.

20

'All Hands to the Pump'

ROSEMARY went back to the cockatoo. He was sitting hunched on his perch with his feathers fluffed out and his eyes closed.

'Can you think of something I can do?' she asked him. 'I must have that particular kitten most specially, and when you aren't, well, giving your public what it wants, you seem so wise.'

The cockatoo opened his eyes. He seemed not displeased. Then he said, 'Excuse me!' sidled to the other end of his perch and made a popping noise like a cork being pulled out, followed by a sound like water coming out of a bottle. All this was for the benefit of a small girl with an elderly woman. Then he sidled back again.

'So many demands on my time – that's the worst of being a public figure,' he said languidly, but keeping a sharp lookout for anyone else who might watch him perform. 'Now then, your little problem. Let me think.'

His grey wrinkled lids lowered over his bright eyes, and Rosemary was afraid he was asleep. But he suddenly sat up, shrieked, 'Whoops-a-daisy!' and hanging from his perch with his black beak, turned a somersault. Then, once more as grave as a professor, he said, 'I've got it, and it will make a very touching performance. Now listen to me. Do you see the fifth link of the chain from the collar on my leg?' Rosemary looked.

'It's very thin,' she said.

'Precisely,' said the bird. 'It took me six months to do it. Every twenty years or so I plan a little excursion.'

'You mean you escape?'

'Bless you, no! I always come back again, but it breaks the monotony. Do you think you could snap that link?'

The only people near were an old man with two children who were choosing a canary. They were far too occupied to notice Rosemary put up her hand to the chain. The link was so thin that it broke with hardly any pressure.

'I was waiting for a really good audience,' said the cockatoo, 'but I'm willing to oblige you this afternoon. You're not used to these public performances, I dare say, but I'm sure they'll make allowances. Now, go over there and talk to your kitten. You'd better not be near me. No one must guess it's a double act, so watch out for the signal.'

Rosemary felt it was no use asking questions, though she would like to have asked what the signal would be. However, she did as she was told. She went across to Pergamond, and had barely explained what had happened to John and Calidor when there was a screech from the cockatoo.

'Polly put the kettle on!' he screamed. 'Oops-a-daisy!' And with a flutter of wings he left his perch and flew to the top of the highest cage in the shop, noisily clanking his broken chain. With his feathers fluffed up he bowed repeatedly, and demanded from the delighted audience below, 'How de do? How de do? How de do?'

The animals set up an excited yapping, mewing, barking and twittering. Only the tortoise went on quietly eating his lettuce. A number of people had come in to see what the laughter was about, and Mr Bodkin poked his head through the bead curtain. When he saw the cockatoo he gasped, and, pushing his way through the crowd, said under his breath, 'Please to keep quiet – a most valuable bird – no sudden movement please or you may startle it!' Then, raising a cautious hand, 'Cockie! Cockie! Good Cockie!' he said anxiously.

'Put a sock in it! Put a sock in it!' said Cockie, and emptied three imaginary bottles in quick succession.

Forgetting Mr Bodkin's warning, the little knot of people below shouted with laughter, and at the sudden noise the bird fluttered from the top of the cage to the top of the open window which looked over the yard. With yellow crest pushed forward he danced like a boxer waiting for an opening.

'All hands to the pump!' he shrieked, and then in his professor voice that only the animals and Rosemary understood, 'Well, what are you waiting for, girl? Get on with it. Turn right outside the shop and down the alley into the yard, and hurry up about it or someone else will catch me. What do you think I'm doing this for? No feeling for drama, you haven't!'

Rosemary had forgotten for a moment that she was anything but part of the audience which was rapidly swelling to a small crowd, but she pulled herself together, slipped out of the shop and down the alleyway into the yard. Through the window she was just in time to see Mr Bodkin give a sudden grab at the cockatoo's dangling chain. With an outraged squawk Cockie flew out into the yard.

He landed on top of a tall, empty crate a few feet away from Rosemary.

'Perhaps it's just as well you didn't buy me,' he said. 'I should probably moult in private life. Give me only a small audience and it goes to my head.'

There was the sound of running footsteps coming down the alley. 'You see how it is? A sought-after public figure – can't call my life my own!' he went on in an affected voice.

Mr Bodkin, fired by some idea of climbing through the window, had stuck half way.

'You there! Catch him! Don't let him escape!' he called to Rosemary. 'Five shillings reward if you'll only get him!'

Rosemary made a grab and was within an ace of catching the chain, but Cockie whisked it away just in time.

'Don't you dare!' he said, and squawked indignantly as he sidled away from her along the crate.

'What do you mean?' asked Rosemary in bewilderment. 'I thought you wanted me to catch you!'

'At five shillings? Insulting I call it! Don't you dare do it until you've beaten him up to fifteen shillings at the very least.'

'Oh dear!' thought Rosemary. The bird by this time was sitting on the gutter of the outhouse that stood in a corner of the yard, which now was full of people. The crowd laughed and chattered and offered advice.

'Dora!' called Mr Bodkin to the overalled assistant who was also in the yard. 'Fetch a ladder!'

Several people went off with her to find one. Cautiously, Cockie clambered first onto the roof, and then up onto the coping which edged the gable end.

Rosemary was already pushing the crate up against

the outhouse wall. By climbing onto the top of it, she was level with the gutter at the edge of the roof. 'I hope to goodness it will hold me,' she said to herself anxiously.

'Good girl!' called Mr Bodkin excitedly. 'Go carefully, go carefully! Ten shillings if you do it.'

The gutter held as she put her weight on it. Slowly and painfully Rosemary pulled herself up the roof by holding onto the coping stone, but as she advanced, Cockie warily climbed higher. Once she slipped and the crowd below gasped.

'He said ... ten shillings,' pleaded Rosemary breathlessly. 'Let me ... catch you ... Cockie! I could ... buy my kitten now!'

'And what about me?' said the cockatoo. 'Ten shillings indeed! I've got my pride. Not a penny under fifteen. You're doing quite nicely. Just keep on, but don't look down!'

The bird had reached the ridge of the roof by now, and like an actor in the centre of the stage he fluffed out his feathers, bowed repeatedly to the crowd, and while he did a shuffling kind of dance screeched, 'Polly put the kettle on! All hands to the pump! How de do? How de do? How de do?' Then he pulled half a dozen corks. The people below laughed and clapped and Cockie bowed again. He was clearly having the time of his life.

Mr Bodkin called anxiously, 'Take care! Take care! Fifteen shillings if you catch him now!'

It was then that Rosemary made the mistake of looking down. She saw the faces tilted up to watch her and the hard paving stones of the yard a long way below, and for the first time she realized how high she was. Hastily she looked away, but the damage was done. Her knees began to shake and her inside suddenly felt as though it was not there.

'Cockie! I can't!' she said faintly. She could feel her feet slipping slowly on the tiles. She gave a frantic lurch, clutched with both hands, and found that one of them had gripped the ridge of the roof, and the other had caught the cockatoo's broken chain. The crowd gasped and cheered as though they were at the circus, as painfully she pulled herself astride the ridge.

'Not bad. Not bad at all. I didn't think you had it in you,' said Cockie from his perch on her shoulder. Then he bowed to the clapping crowd and screamed, 'Put a sock in it!'

By this time Dora and her helpers had arrived with the ladder. They pushed it up onto the roof with the bottom end fixed against the gutter, and Rosemary thankfully clambered down. When she reached the edge of the roof, willing hands helped her to the ground. The crowd patted her on the back and told her how brave she was, and Rosemary wished they would go away. Presently they did, and Mr Bodkin and Dora took her into the shop by a side door. They put Cockie back on his perch and they bathed Rosemary's scraped knees and let her wash her hands, which were quite black. Then Mr Bodkin said, 'I can't thank you enough, my dear. You are a very brave girl. Worth his weight in gold to me, that bird. Brings no end of people to the shop. Would you know what to do with a pound note if I gave it to you?'

'Oh yes!' said Rosemary. 'I should buy the tortoise-shell kitten in the cage at the back of the shop.'

Mr Bodkin laughed, but he fetched Pergamond, and because Rosemary's hands were full of purring, tortoise-shell kitten, he slipped a ten shilling note and

two half crowns as well into the pocket of her gingham dress.

'Take care of the kitten. It's a good one,' he said.

'I will! Oh, I will!' she answered feelingly. Cockie
was sitting on his perch putting his feathers in order.

'Good-bye!' she said. 'And thank you!'

'Put a sock in it!' said the bird, but unnoticed by
Mr Bodkin one grey eye had come down in an unmistakable wink.

21

Dossy

WHEN Rosemary reached home she took Pergamond straight upstairs.

'Why darling, where have you been? I was beginning to grow anxious,' said Mrs Brown.

'I've found one of the kittens, Mother. It's Pergamond.'

'Rosie, I'm so glad!' said her mother.

'May I keep her upstairs with us, just for the night?' begged Rosemary. 'John said he didn't think he'd be back until tomorrow, and she would be company for me. Besides, I shouldn't sleep a wink if she was in the greenhouse. You see she was stolen and sold to a pet shop. I found her there!'

Mrs Brown listened with astonishment while Rosemary told her story, leaving out the magic bits and the complimentary remarks of Mr Bodkin and the crowd of people.

'I've got a present for you,' she ended. 'A box of peppermint creams.'

'My favourite!' said Mrs Brown, and by a lucky chance they were Rosemary's favourite too.

'I'm just going down to tell Woppit about Pergamond,' she said rather indistinctly, because of course her mother had offered her a peppermint cream.

Mrs Brown laughed. 'Don't be long, dear, supper is nearly ready.'

Woppit was sitting brooding in the greenhouse, with her paws tucked in, so that she looked like a rather untidy foot warmer. She had never ceased to reproach herself for the loss of the kittens. When she heard that Pergamond was safe and that at least they knew where Calidor was, she became a different animal. Her purr was like tearing calico, and she rubbed herself against Rosemary's legs with such force that she nearly knocked her over.

'So I thought you had better go and tell Queen Blandamour straight away,' ended Rosemary. 'Or would you like your supper first?'

'As if I'd let bite or sup pass my lips!' said Woppit, 'before I told her Majesty the blessed news! Not that I couldn't fancy something tasty when I get back, mind. A nice bit of liver, minced medium fine, wouldn't come amiss.'

Rosemary watched the untidy old animal leap to the top of the garden wall with surprising ease, and run along it till she was out of sight. Then she went back to the flat.

'All the same, I do wish I knew what was happening to John,' she whispered to Pergamond, who was warming her overfull stomach by the fire, for the evening was chilly.

From the back seat of the car, John had looked through the window behind him at the dwindling figure of Rosemary, as she stood outside the pet shop. She looked rather forlorn standing there by herself on the edge of the pavement, so he waved, until he remembered that she could not see him.

'It wouldn't make any difference to her if I stood on my head!' he said gloomily to himself.

He turned round and studied the backs of the three heads in front of him. There was Dossy's father

with a bowler and a red sort of neck that suggested he
was not a very patient sort of person; there was Dossy's
mother with carefully waved, blue hair under the
very fashionable hat; there was Dossy's own sleek, fair
head in between with the kitten on her shoulder.
Calidor was looking rather miserably over the back of
the seat, unaware that help was so near. Very carefully
John put his mouth as near to the kitten as he could
and whispered, 'Cheer up, it's me, John! I'm in the
back of the car. You can't see me because I'm invisible!'

Calidor started, and to keep his balance stuck his
claws into Dossy's shoulder. Dossy shrieked.

'For goodness' sake!' said her father irritably. He
did not care for sudden squeals when he was driving
through busy traffic.

'He scratched me, Mother!' said Dossy tearfully,
and lifting the kitten onto her knee gave him a slap.
It was not a hard slap, but it upset his balance again
so that once more he had to dig in his claws to prevent
himself from falling off.

Once more Dossy shrieked.

'For mercy's sake put that cat in the back where it
can't scratch you!' said her father crossly.

'It's a horrible kitten!' complained Dossy, dropping
Calidor into the back of the car. 'It scratched me twice!
I wish I'd chosen the ginger one!'

'I wish you'd chosen a goldfish. At least that couldn't
scratch,' growled her father.

'Now, Charlie!' said Dossy's mother. 'The poor
child must have something to amuse her while the
television is out of order.'

John ignored the argument that seemed to be starting in the front seat, and putting Calidor on the rug

which lay folded beside him, whispered. 'It's all right, Calidor, I'll get you out of here somehow. You needn't be afraid.'

'I'm not afraid . . . exactly,' said Calidor stoutly. 'But it does make it easier to be brave, now you're here.'

He snuggled up against John's invisible grey flannel shorts, and after giving a few halfhearted licks to his shirt front to show how self-possessed he was, under John's stroking fingers he fell asleep. The powerful car had slipped with surprising speed out of the town and into the kind of suburb which has big houses built in large gardens.

'I hope to goodness they aren't going for miles and miles,' said John to himself.

He was relieved to hear Dossy's father say, 'Nearly home. You'll be pretty late for tea, Doss. I thought you were expecting someone?'

'Good heavens, I'd clean forgotten! But I dare say it doesn't matter,' said his wife comfortably.

'It's only Milly,' said Dossy in a bored voice. 'I expect she'll come in that awful old blue cotton frock again.'

'I think it's the only best one she has. You musn't give yourself airs, darling, because you are a lucky little girl with lots of pretty things!' said her mother.

'She seems a nice kid to me. Plenty of go in her,' said Dossy's father. 'I can't think why you don't like her.'

'She always wants to play such silly games,' said Dossy. 'Wanting to pretend something or other all the time.'

John decided at once that he, too, would like Milly.

'Well, don't forget she's your guest, darling,' said Dossy's mother. 'You must play her games, too. I sometimes wonder if you don't have a teeny, weeny bit too much of your own way. Look, there is Milly!'

'She's sitting on our gate!' said Dossy. 'And she *is* wearing that old blue thing.'

As the car drew up, Milly jumped down and opened the gate for them. She was a plump person with short red hair, and a great many freckles.

'I got tired of waiting inside,' she explained. 'I was pretending I was a cowboy.'

Dossy sniffed, but her father chuckled. 'Hop in the back, Milly, and we'll give you a ride up the drive.'

John had barely time to squeeze himself into a corner before she got in.

'You haven't noticed our new car!' said Dossy in a huffy voice. But Milly might not have heard. She had eyes for nothing but Calidor. 'What a darling kitten! What's his name? Where did he come from?'

'He's mine ... because ... because I was good at the dentist's.' Dossy had the grace to go rather red as she said this. 'I don't like him very much,' she went on. 'He scratched me twice, and he hasn't purred once.'

'Perhaps he hasn't anything to purr about. Can we go to the kitchen and get him some milk?'

'Mrs Parkin doesn't like children bothering around in the kitchen,' said Dossy's mother firmly. 'He shall have some at tea time. Here we are. Now run along in and wash your hands.'

John was determined not to let Calidor out of his sight. He followed the two girls into the house, narrowly missing getting himself slammed in the door of the car by the unsuspecting Milly. Dossy carried Calidor. They took him with them into the bathroom, which was panelled with black marble and pink trimmings. John followed. His hands were so dirty that he tried to wash them, too, but Dossy pulled the plug out before he had finished. The dirty marks on the pink towel were blamed on Milly. Next he followed them to Dossy's bedroom, so that Milly could be shown her new party dress. It was all rather embarrassing, because he felt he was eavesdropping, so he was relieved when a gong interrupted and they went downstairs to tea. Calidor came down on Milly's shoulder, wobbling uncomfortably as she bounced from step to step. His ears were flattened crossly.

'I've got legs of my own, haven't I? Why can't they put me down?' he muttered to John following closely behind.

'Well, at least you'll get your saucer of milk,' whispered John. 'I shan't get anything at all!'

This time it was almost more than John could bear. There were a great many little sandwiches and delicious cakes. They sat on low chairs, and Milly found it difficult to manage a very small plate on her knee, a lace-edged napkin, a cream horn and a special fork to eat it with. Luckily for John, half the cream horn slid onto the floor. Although he would have hesitated to take a cake from the table, which would be like stealing, he felt that half a cream horn on the floor was different, and he picked it up and ate it thankfully. Milly was equally thankful to find it was not there when she looked furtively down, though she was rather puzzled.

Calidor lapped milk politely from a china saucer in a way that would have warmed the heart of Woppit. He even remembered 'to purr his grace'.

After tea the two girls were sent into the garden to play. They scooped up the indignant Calidor from the cushion on which he had settled down to sleep, and Dossy's mother called after them, 'Milly's games this time, darling!'

22

The Queen of Sheba

It was a beautiful garden. Leaving the flower beds behind, the two girls, with John close behind them, ran down the lawn which sloped toward a small lake. It lay cool and still in the evening light. The reflections of the trees which grew on the farther side were only broken by the fish that occasionally rose with a little 'plop'. John could not quite catch what they said as they leaped from the shining surface. A blackbird perched on a willow tree sang a song to the praise of summer evenings, and this evening in particular.

The girls made their way to a little paved terrace with stone steps which led down into the water where a punt lay moored invitingly. The name *Swallow* was painted on her side.

'Let's go in it!' said Milly.

'I'm not allowed to, not without a grown-up, until I can swim. It's my turn to carry the kitten!' said Dossy, and she took him clumsily from Milly's shoulder.

'Why can't they leave me alone?' grumbled Calidor. His whiskers were at sixes and sevens and his fur was ruffled.

There was a clump of foxgloves growing by the boathouse. Milly picked up two fallen flowers and perched one on each of the kitten's ears. He looked so funny that they both laughed. Calidor twitched the flowers off angrily.

'Funny, am I?' he growled furiously. 'Well, I've got claws I have, and if you don't –'

'Steady on, Calidor!' said John. 'Stick it out until we can get away. We've got to wait our chance.'

'Let's play something,' said Milly. 'Let's pretend –'

'Oh, no!' broke in Dossy. 'Well, I suppose we must if you want to,' she went on. 'Mother said I had to play your games this time.'

'Don't you ever pretend anything?' asked Milly curiously.

There was a pause, then Dossy said, 'Only one thing, sometimes.' She flushed. 'Promise you won't laugh if I tell you?'

'Promise!'

'Well, sometimes I pretend I'm the best-dressed girl in Broomhurst.'

'Gosh, how ghastly!' said Milly frankly. 'I'm not laughing, honestly I'm not,' she went on hurriedly. 'I say, I know a gorgeous game we could play. Let's pretend you're the Queen of Sheba! She was the best-dressed woman in the Bible, at least I think she was, and she was very beautiful, and she came sailing down the Nile – that could be the lake – to see King Solomon because of his wisdom – that would be me – and brought him rare gifts.'

'But I don't –' began Dossy.

'You go and dress up. I'm sure you can find some queenly things somewhere, old ones of your mother's. There are some striped towels in the boathouse which will do beautifully for me!' Milly said.

Dossy pushed the kitten into Milly's arms and then she ran, quite quickly, back to the house. John watched Milly rather enviously. Humming between her teeth, she investigated the bathing things in the boathouse.

This was just the sort of game he would have enjoyed playing himself. In fact, he was so interested that he forgot to seize the opportunity to pick up Calidor and make off. Instead he watched Milly. First she put the kitten in the punt to keep him safe. He put his paws on the gunwale and peered over the side. 'Water!' he said with disgust, and dropped back hastily onto the cushions.

Next, Milly put on a magnificently patterned bathing wrap belonging to Dossy's father. It was much too large for her – he was a big man – so she tied a cushion on underneath to fill it out. 'More dignified if I look fatter, too,' she said to herself. Then she took a bathing towel and twisted it around her head into a turban.

When she had done this, she took out a folding chair, and with some difficulty, because of her trailing robe and the tied-on cushion, set it on the flat nose of the punt. Then she draped another towel over the chair and filled the seat with cushions. The remaining cushions she piled in the punt. Calidor, recovered from his sulks, happily chased the trailing cord of King Solomon's robe. John could not resist tweaking a towel here, and a cushion there, to help arrange things. It really did look rather oriental, he thought. They were all so busy that they did not hear Dossy's return.

'Will I do?' she said suddenly behind them.

They turned around.

Instead of putting on some old dress of her mother's as Milly expected, she was wearing her new party frock. From its high waist, the skirt, scattered with shining beads, fell in a blue cascade to her silver slippers. Her pale gold hair, loosened from its ponytail, fell on to her shoulders, and was held in place on the top of her head by a sparkling necklace of her mother's, which she wore as a shimmering crown. A wide silver scarf pinned to her shoulders billowed behind her as she walked. Her pale cheeks were flushed.

'Dossy! You are beautiful!' said Milly in an awed voice.

Even John said to himself, 'She doesn't look half bad.'

Milly stood up and bowed as low as she could over the cushions.

'Welcome, O Queen of Sheba!' she said. 'Your royal barge awaits you! Behold your throne!'

She waved, with dignity, toward the folding chair on the end of the punt.

The Queen of Sheba stepped carefully down, narrowly missing John as she landed.

Milly went on, 'Now, you say, "O Solomon, live forever!"'

'O Solomon, live forever!' repeated Dossy obediently.

Solomon took the hand of the Queen of Sheba and, stumbling a little over the trailing robe, led her to the 'throne' on the end of the punt.

The Queen of Sheba sat down gingerly.

'Now you say, "O King, I bring you precious gifts!"' She paused. 'Go on, say it!'

'But I don't. I haven't brought you anything,' said Dossy.

'Well, give me the kitten then. You can pretend it isn't an ordinary cat but some strange, rare animal.'

She bundled Calidor onto Dossy's lap. His ruffled head appeared with a protesting 'mew!' among the blue folds of the party dress.

'An ordinary cat indeed! Me, a kitten of the royal

blood! I dare say –' began Calidor. But John heard no
more, for the Queen of Sheba flung the 'rare
animal' back again to King Solomon. In her anxiety
lest he should catch his claws in the blue dress, she had
not noticed that she was holding him upside down.

King Solomon turned to the imaginary oarsmen of
the royal barge and waved imperiously, 'To your oars,
men, and row us to the Palace of a Thousand Jewels!'

Milly really did it very well, thought John, and
quite carried away he pulled the painter free and gave
a vigorous shove off. The punt shot out into the lake.

'Whatever have you done?' gasped Dossy.

Milly looked puzzled.

'I didn't do anything – I was only pretending. I
didn't really mean the barge to move. It must have
been a current or something. But there's no need to
panic. We can punt ourselves back again.'

She looked for the pole.

'I told you I wasn't allowed to use the punt, and I
shall get into frightful trouble for putting on my party
frock as well!' wailed Dossy. 'And if Mother's silver
scarf gets splashed she'll be simply furious. Perhaps if
we get home quickly I can put the things back without anyone knowing!'

Milly looked up and her face was worried.

'I'm awfully sorry. The punt pole isn't here, or the
paddles either!' she said. 'I don't see how we can get
back.'

Dossy burst into tears. 'I think this is a beastly game.
It's all this silly pretending,' she wailed.

'It was rather queer, the barge sailing off when I
told it to,' said Milly uneasily.

John felt thoroughly uncomfortable. He would have
liked to explain that it was all his fault and nothing to

do with Milly's pretending, but of course that was not possible.

The punt slowed down at last until it ceased to move. The little slapping waves beneath their bows grew fainter and fainter until they died away altogether.

'It's not really so bad,' said Milly. 'They'll be sure to come and look for us soon. Let's fill in time by playing something else. Oh, look, fish! Did you see that one leap right out, over there! Let's pretend it's an enchanted lake and that there is a sea serpent living in its fathomless depths!'

'Oh, let's not!' sniffed Dossy, looking round nervously. She was still sitting huddled in the throne on the end of the punt. The shadows of the trees were lengthening over the lake. Suddenly a fish leaped from the water so near that Dossy, who was thinking uneasily of sea serpents, gave a startled gasp and jumped to her feet, pushing the chair back as she did so. Milly made a grab to stop it falling overboard, but catching her foot in her trailing robe, she lurched and fell heavily against Dossy, who gave a piercing shriek. For a moment they tottered on the edge together, then with a tremendous splash the two girls, and the chair, fell into the water. The punt lurched dangerously.

'Out of the way!' said John to Calidor, who was peering over with great interest. 'Dossy can't swim – I'm going in after her!'

There was a splash which showered the watching kitten, and a sudden cleft in the water which showed where John must have dived. Calidor could see the Queen of Sheba's throne bobbing up and down half out of the water, accompanied by three, sodden cushions. Then Milly's spluttering head appeared above the surface.

'It's all right, Dossy, it's not deep!' she gasped, looking anxiously around. She was relieved to see Dossy's head appear, but only long enough to let out another shriek before it disappeared again.

Milly paddled frantically toward the widening circle of ripples which showed where Dossy had surfaced, and then a curious sight made her draw up and tread water. Dossy's head had come to the surface again, and apparently with nothing to account for it, a series of small splashes, followed by what looked like a miniature tidal wave bore down upon her. Milly, of course, had no idea that it was caused by the swimming of the invisible John. She was only aware that the steadily screaming Dossy rose half out of the water, made her way back to the punt without showing any signs of swimming and, as though pushed up by some submarine volcano, rose in a surge of foam and tumbled on to the floor of the *Swallow*.

Milly had no time to wonder. She was hanging onto the edge of the punt by now. She had managed to rid herself of the hampering folds of the bathing wrap, but with the waterlogged cushion still tied to her waist, she had not the strength to pull herself up.

'Help!' she called forlornly, and as though in response something seemed to give her a great heave from below, and she fell thankfully beside Dossy in the bottom of the punt. For a minute she lay there panting, then slowly she sat up. Dossy lay sobbing in a pool of water. The party frock was ruined, its sodden folds streaked with water weed. The shining crown was gone and the silver scarf lay torn and muddy beside her.

'It's all your fault, Milly!' she sobbed. 'First you pretended the boat was going to move, and it did. Then you pretended the lake was enchanted, and it was. It must be. I felt someone lift me up and push me into the punt, and there wasn't anyone there at all. Well, you'd better pretend somebody to push us back to the steps or we shall both die from double pneumonia!' Dossy lay down and cried again.

Milly swallowed hard. She had to admit it had been rather odd, and there was the mysterious heave that something had given her when she found she could not climb back into the punt.

'I suppose it might have been the sea serpent I imagined,' she said to herself, looking nervously over the side.

She pushed a strand of dripping hair out of her eyes and said, 'Let's pretend the punt will take us back to the landing stage of its own accord.'

At once the punt began to move, not very fast, it is true, and certainly not fast enough to explain the curious splashing in its wake. The two girls sat up, still and silent, as it glided on, but the minute the *Swallow* touched the steps they leaped out. Dossy raced up the sloping grass to the house faster than she had ever run before. John heard her diminishing cries of 'Mummy! Mummy!' as she disappeared. Milly followed more slowly.

When they had gone, he tied up the punt, climbed wearily up the steps on to the terrace and flung himself on the ground.

23

Milly

FOR a few minutes John lay panting on the flagstones. They were still warm, although the sun was no longer shining on them. It had been hard work heaving two well-grown girls out of the water, and pushing the punt back to its moorings immediately afterwards had taken all his strength. Suddenly he felt a small rasping tongue lick his cheek. It was Calidor. The kitten could see where John lay by the shape of the rapidly growing puddle beneath him.

'You *must* have got your paws wet!' said Calidor sympathetically.

'Hello, Calidor!' said John, opening his eyes. 'Have they left you behind?'

Calidor sniffed.

'One minute they can't leave me alone, and the next I might be an old punt cushion for all they care about me!'

John sat up.

'What a stroke of luck!' he said. 'Now's our chance to get away. But talking of punt cushions, I suppose it was all my fault. I think I ought to salvage what I can before we go. I can't get much wetter.'

Calidor watched with interest the growing chain of wet footmarks – the only sign of John's progress back to the edge of the lake. He listened to the splash of John's dive, and then turned his attention to washing his ruffled black coat.

It took John longer than he expected to collect the

floating properties of the royal barge. One of the cushions had foundered, and he had to give up his search, but three others, the chair and King Solomon's turban he left to dry on the terrace. Then he went into the boathouse to look for a towel with which to dry himself as much as possible before starting home. He felt very tired, rather cold in his wet clothes and extremely hungry, but the knowledge that Calidor was as good as recovered made it all worth while. He was in the boathouse giving himself a hard rub down and wondering how on earth they were going to get back to Fallowhithe, when Calidor, who was sitting beside him, suddenly said, 'Look out! Here's one of 'em back again!'

It was Milly, wearing one of Dossy's old frocks. It looked uncomfortably tight.

'Pussy!' she called. 'Puss! puss! puss!'

Calidor backed into a corner of the boathouse, but the movement attracted her attention.

'Oh, there you are! Come along, pusskin!'

She advanced toward the kitten with her hand held out, and, I am sorry to say, Calidor spat. Milly laughed and knelt down so that he was penned into the corner.

'It's no good being cross, because you're mine now, darling! Dossy says she's tired of you. Come along. Mr Dawson is waiting to take us home. Everybody is so cross already that I don't think we'd better keep him waiting!'

She picked up Calidor.

'Help!' he mewed. 'Help, help!'

John's heart sank. To be on the brink of success only to find the kitten being carried off by another owner!

Milly was leaving the boathouse with the kitten in her arms. There was no time to think of any plan.

'Milly!' called John in desperation. 'Don't go!'

She turned around in surprise. Standing outside in the bright summer evening she could see nothing but shadows inside the boathouse, so that the fact she could not distinguish the speaker did not surprise her.

'Who's there?' she asked.

'John, but you wouldn't know me. I want your help. No, don't come in. I, I've got no clothes on. I'm drying. I've just fished all the cushions and the chair out of the lake.'

'Gosh, thanks awfully!' said Milly.

'I've hung King Solomon's turban on the stone seat to dry.'

'How do you know about King Solomon?' asked Milly curiously.

'Because I was in the royal barge as well, when Dossy was being the Queen of Sheba. It was me that pushed off,' he went on, regardless of grammar. 'I'm sorry about that. But I did heave you both back into the punt again, and bring it back to the steps.'

Milly opened her eyes very wide. 'Then it wasn't my pretending come true! Thank goodness! It was horrible thinking that every time I said "Let's pretend", it would really happen. You can't think how bothered I've been. But look here, you couldn't have done it. I should have seen you!'

'That's the trouble,' said John. 'Now don't go having hysterics or anything, but I'm invisible.'

'Not really!' said Milly with deep interest. She peered into the boathouse, but she could see nobody there. 'You're hiding!' she said at last.

'No, I'm not!' said a voice in the empty air beside her.

Milly jumped so violently that she dropped Calidor.

'You'll soon get used to the idea,' said the voice, this time from the other side. 'It's the kitten I've come for.

He really belongs to me and my friend Rosemary. Someone stole him and sold him to a pet shop, and when Dossy bought him I got in the car and came with them. If you don't believe I'm invisible, look at the kitten. I'm going to pick him up.'

Milly watched enthralled while Calidor rose gently in the air, his furry body hanging limply, as it might over a lifting hand. She rubbed her eyes.

'It's no good. I don't know what's pretend and what isn't. Anything could happen this afternoon. I almost think I do believe you. You said you wanted me to help you. What shall I do?'

'Give me the kitten!' said John.

'Is that all!' said Milly with relief. 'As a matter of fact I'd be rather glad. When Dossy said would I like him, I quite forgot Mother said she couldn't put up with one single more pet. The boys and I have so many, and I was wondering what she'd say when I turned up with this one. Besides, you did save us both this afternoon. But look here. Mr Dawson is taking me home in the car. I live at Fiddleworth. Daddy is rector of St Mary's Church.

'You will have to come in the car with us and as soon as Mr Dawson has gone I'll hand the kitten over again.'

They walked back up the sloping lawn, Calidor purring happily and thrusting the top of his small, sleek head against John's chin.

'What's happened to Dossy?' asked John.

'Bed,' said Milly shortly, 'with hot water bottles and aspirins. She was still moaning when I left.'

'Were they very angry?'

'Mrs Dawson was, especially about the new dress. Mr Dawson was wonderful. He laughed, and said we had overdone it a bit this time, but that Dossy needed a bit of shaking up. All the same, I don't think I shall be asked to play again somehow.'

John was inclined to agree.

24

The Counter-Spell

IT must have been about midnight when Rosemary was woken up by someone shaking her shoulder.

'Wake up, Rosie!' whispered an urgent voice. 'Wake up!'

She struggled sleepily out of the ball in which she always curled herself when she went to sleep, and sat up, suddenly wide awake.

'John, is it you? Have you got Calidor?'

'I've got him right enough,' said John, and a furry, purring pressure against her side confirmed it.

'Oh, Calidor, I'm so glad!'

She picked up the kitten and hugged him. 'Now we've got you both safely back, and we needn't worry about you any more!'

'Well, you can just start worrying about me instead!' said John, and he made the unmistakable noise of someone trying to suppress a heavy sneeze.

'I've got an awful cold, through going about in soaking clothes. I'll tell you all about it later. I don't want to be invisible for one minute longer. We've got to work out the counter-spell – now! If I'm going to be ill, how on earth can a doctor sound my chest if he can't see it?' he went on gloomily.

Rosemary jumped out of bed with the kitten in her arms.

'As a matter of fact, I remembered about the counter-spell, I got all the things ready just in case,' she said as she laid Calidor gently down in the box at the foot of her bed, where Pergamond lay sleeping. 'I had to do something to keep myself from worrying about you. It's all under the bed.'

The white shape that was Rosemary's nightgown went on its knees by the bed and dragged something out from beneath. When John switched on the light, he saw it was a large tin tray. In the centre was one acid drop, an empty eggshell and a candle end. At least that was all that Rosemary could see. John could also see the book of magic and the saucepan that had held the invisible mixture.

'Good old Rosie!' said John.

'I cleaned the saucepan as best I could with wire wool,' went on Rosemary. 'You'd better check up on everything from the book because of course I couldn't read it. I think it would be all right to brew it in the kitchen – Mother's room is at the other end of the passage. I don't think she'd hear.'

They crept into the kitchen and put the tray on the table.

Rosemary heard the sound of pages being hastily turned.

'Here we are! "Counter-spell of Invisibility",' he read. 'Now then,' he went on in a preoccupied voice, 'it says, "the moon must be on the wane". Well, that's all right, I noticed when I was coming home. And it must be done in the original saucepan. That's all right, too. Now then, "Put in the saucepan or pipkin seven eggshells full of water, so clear that it doth appear not to be there." You couldn't have anything much clearer than Fallowhithe District Council's tap water, so here goes!'

Rosemary watched while apparently unaided the

eggshell filled itself seven times from the tap over the sink, and seven times emptied itself into what she guessed must be the invisible saucepan.

'"And in it place some transparent substance that by boiling will consume itself,"' he read. 'Is that what the acid drop is for?'

'It's nearly transparent, and it will melt when the water boils,' said Rosemary and dropped it in the water.

'"Then, by the light of a dwindled candle –"' went on John.

Rosemary stood the candle end in a saucer which she put on the plate rack above the cooker, and lit it with a match.

'If it goes on dwindling too quickly I shan't be able to see to read the incantation, so hurry up and light the gas under the saucepan.'

There was a plop as the ring of blue gas jets shot out, and curled around the bottom of the saucepan.

'Here's a spoon to stir it with,' said Rosemary. 'I looked up "widdershins" in the dictionary and it said it meant counterclockwise.' She tactfully did not point out that that was what she had said in their unfortunate argument that morning.

John turned off the light, and at once the trim little kitchen was filled with the dark, wavering shadows cast by the candle flame. Already they could see by a ring of bubbles that the water was beginning to boil. Then the acid drop began to leap and bounce on the bottom of the pan. The water boiled furiously, and as it boiled it began to evaporate, and the dancing acid drop grew smaller and smaller and smaller. John watched, fascinated.

'Go on! Stir, and intone the incantation!' said Rosemary.

It is not easy to stir a saucepan widdershins and read aloud from cramped, old-fashioned writing by the light of a guttering candle end, but John managed somehow. This is what he intoned:

> *'Vapours curdle and congeal,*
> *Shadows thicken and reveal*
> *Solid shapes to see and feel!*
>   *Hocus pocus*
>   *Into focus,*
> *Invisibility – repeal!'*

As he said the word 'repeal' the spoon twisted itself from his hand and fell with a clatter to the floor; the last drop of moisture dried up in the pan with a sizzle, and by the light of the candle, which suddenly flared up, Rosemary saw a strange sight. She was standing staring where she knew John must be, in front of the cooker, between herself and the kitchen dresser. And as the candle flared up she saw a pale, shadowy form begin to appear. She could see through it the knobs on the dresser drawer and the cups hanging on their hooks, but as she watched, the cups and the knobs grew fainter and fainter and the shape of John more solid. Then the candle went out as suddenly as it had flared up.

'Put the light on, Rosie!' said John in a matter-of-fact voice.

She rushed to the switch, and as the prosaic light from the hanging bulb flooded the little kitchen, she saw John standing there, firm, untransparent, hair on end and dirtier than she had ever seen him, but visible.

'Am I all right again?' he asked anxiously.

'Right as rain!' said Rosemary beaming from ear to ear, and she seized his nearest hand and shook it up

and down like a pump handle to show how pleased she was.

A sudden smell of burning sugar made them look round. The gas was full on under the empty saucepan, which was now visible for anyone to see. So was the book which John had propped up against the kettle behind the lighted ring. Whether the change to visibility had affected its balance, I do not know, but it had fallen forward on its face, with the blue flame of the lighted ring licking at one corner; already the ancient paper, dry as tinder, was well alight.

'Quick, put it in the sink and turn the tap on it!' said Rosemary.

John picked up the book and rushed across to the sink, and as he ran, the wind of his going fanned the flames so that they streamed behind him. Twisting red, green and purple flames sent out a shower of many coloured sparks, and though the sparks fell on John's face and hands, he did not feel them. Rosemary had already run to the sink where she had put in the plug and turned both taps full on. As the book fell in the water with a hiss, a column of jagged purple flame shot up to the ceiling and went out, leaving nothing behind but a little plume of oily, evil-smelling smoke.

'What queer-looking flames!' said Rosemary.

'Well, it was a queer sort of book!' said John.

The charred remains of the book bobbed sluggishly up and down in the sink. He lifted it out gingerly.

'The cover isn't too bad,' said Rosemary hopefully. 'But I don't think anyone will be able to read what is left of the inside.'

'I'm glad it's Miss Dibdin who has to take it back to the reference library, and not me!' said John. 'I suppose we'd better keep all there is of it.'

They fished out all they could, and drained it as well as they were able in a colander.

'It can go under my bed till the morning,' said Rosemary. 'But John, I do so want to hear all your adventures!'

John stifled a noise that was half a yawn and half a sneeze. 'All I want is to go to bed and sleep and sleep. I'll tell you about it in the morning. It's been quite a day!'

25

The Green Mixture

ROSEMARY woke early next morning. She tiptoed into John's room and shook him gently but quite firmly.

'Wake up!' she said. 'I'm simply dying to hear about your adventures, and how you rescued Calidor!'

A flushed and tousled John told his story, and Rosemary listened with admiration. 'I got a ride in a lorry back from Fiddleworth,' he ended. 'All the same,' he went on crossly, 'why couldn't you let me have my sleep out in peace?'

'Because if Mother finds you've been having your sleep out in peace in your own bed here, when you are supposed to be staying with your Aunt Annabel, there will have to be some pretty awkward explanations!' said Rosemary, and John had to agree.

They decided that the best plan would be for him to get dressed straight away, go down to the greenhouse and tell Woppit what had happened. Queen Blandamour could then be told as soon as possible that Calidor, too, was safe.

'You had better hide in the Green Cave until after breakfast, and then come and knock on the front door as though you've just arrived,' said Rosemary.

'All right,' said John. 'It couldn't be before breakfast, could it?' he asked wistfully.

'It couldn't,' said Rosemary firmly. 'That would look very suspicious.'

She left John to his dressing and went to make her mother an early morning cup of tea, because she felt uncomfortable about not telling her what had really happened. Magic was like that, she thought regretfully. Luckily Mrs Brown accepted the fact that Calidor had come back without any awkward questions, and she was delighted to see John again when he politely rang the bell when they were washing the breakfast things.

'But my dear boy, what a dreadful cold you've caught!' she said when he sneezed violently.

'I fell id sub water and got awfully wet yesterday. I expect that's what caused it,' said John.

She felt his hot forehead.

'Hm, bed is the best place for you, my dear,' and to Rosemary's surprise, he seemed quite glad to go.

When he was tucked up with a hot water bottle, Mrs Brown said, 'Rosie, you had better get some of that special cold cure from Hedgem and Fudge. It's wonderful stuff. I must get down to the sewing room now. When these Julius Caesar clothes are done I shan't be so busy. I can't think how the Romans managed without sewing machines.'

'I can go and talk to John, can't I?' asked Rosemary anxiously. 'It's a wet-feet kind of cold, not a catching one.'

Her mother smiled. 'All right, darling. Dinner at half past one. You might peel some potatoes before you go.'

When her mother had gone, Rosemary found John some breakfast. First he had some cornflakes while she cooked him some porridge. Then she boiled him two of the largest, brownest eggs in the larder and he finished off with six pieces of toast and marmalade. While he ate she sat beside him and peeled the potatoes on a tray across her knees. When the last crumb had disappeared, John gave a great satisfied sigh and wiggled his toes under the bedclothes, to the delight of the kittens.

'Dow I feel better!' he said, and went on in a snuffly voice, 'I say, I noticed something last night when I was coming home on the back of the lorry. We had to go through the outskirts of Broomhurst, and the whole place was alive with cats. Even the lorry driver noticed. They were running backwards and forwards along the walls and collecting in corners and waste spaces. In one place, it was a church yard I think, there was a whole collection of them, with a great striped brute in front who looked as though he was making a speech.'

'What was he saying?' asked Rosemary.

'I couldn't hear, which isn't surprising, because the lorry was carrying a load of lemonade bottles, and we were doing fifty miles an hour at least!'

'But the Fallowhithe cats –?'

'They were just trotting about their ordinary business. You know, I wonder if Merbeck is right not to warn them what's in the wind?'

'I've been wondering that,' said Rosemary. 'And what I've also been wondering is what is happening about Mrs Flackett's son, Albert. Do you think he is still shutting himself up in his bedroom, refusing to talk to anybody?'

'Well, you'd better set off to Hedgem & Fudge as soon as you can and find out.'

'He may even be back at work again,' said Rosemary hopefully.

But he was not.

When Rosemary reached the chemist shop, Mr Fudge himself was serving behind the medicine counter. There were several customers before her, so she had to wait a little while to be served.

'I'm sorry to keep you waiting, Madam,' he said to a

fat woman who was tapping impatiently on the counter. 'One of my assistants is away ill, so that I'm short-handed. I have another coming next week.'

Another assistant! This meant that Albert was losing his job, and it was all their fault! Rosemary looked across at the perfumery counter where Albert's young lady worked. She looked as though she had been crying.

With the bottle of cold cure safely in her blazer pocket, Rosemary walked thoughtfully out of the shop. If only they could find the counter-spell for the red mixture he had tasted by mistake! She looked up at the shop window. The great cut glass bottle of crimson liquid glowed like a huge ruby. Then she glanced at the other window. There stood the companion bottle, gleaming green and vivid as a great emerald.

'Surely it must be the green liquid which undoes the magic of the red,' thought Rosemary. 'But what if it doesn't? What if it does something quite different, like making you sprout two heads or turn into something creepy crawly? I don't think I'm quite brave enough just to try and see.'

She turned slowly away and walked on down the crowded High Street. She was so deep in thought that she forgot to look where she was going. Suddenly she bumped into someone carrying an overloaded shopping basket. Several packages fell out.

'Oh, I'm so sorry!' said Rosemary, and stooped to collect the fallen things.

As she retrieved a rolling tin of baked beans she noticed the shoes of the owner. They were very large and black with big brass buckles. She looked up quickly. Yes, it was Mrs Cantrip.

'I'm so sorry!' said Rosemary again, rather faintly.

The old woman looked at her from beneath the headscarf she was wearing. It was scarlet, with a pattern of bold black shapes. To Rosemary's surprise she looked almost amiable, so with a rush she said, 'Please, Mrs Cantrip, you remember the prescription you gave us to make us hearing humans?'

'Oh, ah, I remember!' The old woman nodded.

'Well, if you drink the green liquid from the other bottle, will it cancel out the red magic?'

Mrs Cantrip hunched her shoulders and put her head on one side.

'So you've got tired of being a hearing human, have you? Mind, I don't say as I blame you. All that animal chatter, as well as human! I wouldn't be in your shoes when that Carbonel comes back and finds his kittens gone! It might be just as well if you couldn't hear what he says to you.'

Rosemary opened her mouth to say that the kittens were both safe and sound again, but she remembered just in time and said nothing.

'You'd best get out of it all. I don't mind telling you there's more trouble to come! I've got a shot in my locker yet!' And the old woman chuckled.

'But the green liquid?' went on Rosemary.

Mrs Cantrip pursed up her mouth till it looked like a buttonhole and drew in her breath as she considered. At last she said, 'All right, I'll tell you. For why? Because it suits me to, and mind you, magic is the one thing that the likes of me can't lie about, so you needn't be afraid. The answer is yes. The green potion is not so tasty perhaps, but it's good and thorough.'

'Oh, thank you!' said Rosemary gratefully.

'What for?' said Mrs Cantrip sharply. 'Not that it wasn't quick of you to spot it for yourself. I've always thought you aren't so milk and water as you look. That affair with the rocking chair, now, clever that was! I suppose you wouldn't consider taking up the business seriously yourself? I'd take you on as an apprentice!'

Rosemary shook her head hard. The offer seemed almost a kind one, so she did not say what she really felt about it.

'Me, Rosemary Brown, to train as a witch!' she thought indignantly.

'Ah, if you'd seen the ranting, roaring, good old days, maybe you'd think differently,' said the old woman. 'It's the loneliness that makes it so hard nowadays, to be the only one left. Why I've seen as many fly-by-nights on a midsummer's evening as there are smuts in the room when the chimney's been smoking. And the air so full of magic that it fair crackled with it! And I've seen 'em all go out, one by one, like bubbles on a bowl of water.'

The old woman's eyes were dim.

'But Miss Dibdin –' began Rosemary.

'Her?' said Mrs Cantrip with contempt. 'She can't so much as whistle a psalm tune backward! No ear for music. And do you know the only bit of magic she ever pulled off?'

'What?' asked Rosemary.

'A bit of invisibility – child's play. But what does she have to do when half my furniture's vanished?'

'What?' asked Rosemary again, although she thought she knew the answer.

'Why, lose the book with the counter-spell in it, so that I was forever tripping over things I couldn't see. Lucky for her she put it right somehow. It was all there again this morning.'

'How did she do it?' asked Rosemary curiously.

'That's no concern of yours!' snapped Mrs Cantrip. Her softened mood had gone. 'Well, don't keep me gossiping here!' she said, and, hitching her shawl more firmly around her thin shoulders, turned and disappeared among the throng of shoppers, with her basket over her arm.

Rosemary turned and ran as fast as she could back to Hedgem & Fudge. As she reached the shop it was just striking one o'clock. Albert Flackett's young lady was hanging a notice on the door which said 'Closed.'

'Oh please, I must speak to you!' she gasped breathlessly. 'It's about Mr Flackett!'

The young lady, whose name was Myrtle Jones, tossed her flaxen head. 'I'm sure I'm not interested in Albert Flackett!' she said, but the sniff that followed was a sorrowful, not an angry one.

'But surely you don't want him to lose his job?' pleaded Rosemary. 'And him the only son of his mother. Mrs Flackett's so proud of him!'

The girl looked at Rosemary shrewdly for a minute as if undecided.

'Here, come inside,' she said at last.

The pale green light that filtered through the drawn blinds made it seem a mysterious place. The only things that stood out in the gloom were the two huge bottles that stood on the mahogany partition dividing the window from the shop. The crimson of the red bottle was a little dulled by the green light, but the green liquid glowed clearer and brighter than ever above them.

'If it's a message from Albert,' said Myrtle, 'you can just tell him from me –'

'But it's not a message,' said Rosemary. 'He doesn't

know I've come. And please, please don't be angry with him, because it's all our fault!'

'Now if this is some more of his nonsense,' began Myrtle.

'But it isn't! Oh, please listen. Now, do you remember the day he was taken ill, he and Mr Fudge took down the big red bottle out of the window?'

'Yes, yes, I do,' said the girl. 'You could have knocked me down with a feather when I saw them doing it. I've never seen it happen before.' She sat down on one of the chairs provided for the customers.

'Well, that was our prescription, and Albert got it all over his hands when he was pouring it out, and then when he was turning over the pages of the catalogue he kept licking his thumb. Don't you see, that made him ill!'

'Poor Bertie!' said Myrtle in a softened voice. 'But to refuse to see me, after me and him going steady for three years!'

'But if you'll only do what I say, he'll get better, and you can go on going steady.'

'All right, ducks,' said Myrtle suddenly. 'What do you want me to do?'

'Give him a teaspoonful of the green liquid from the other bottle!' said Rosemary. 'I'll get the ladder, while you fetch something to put the mixture in, and a spoon to get it out.'

'Well, things can't be much worse than they are!' said Myrtle. 'Here goes!'

She disappeared behind the glass partition where the dispensing was done. When she came back, Rosemary was already at the top of the steps which she had propped against the partition, and the cut glass stopper of the great bottle was in her hand. A vapour rose from the neck of the bottle, and a sweetish smell which made her head swim filled the darkened shop.

'Please hold the stopper while I fill the little bottle!' said Rosemary.

Very carefully she scooped some of the liquid up with the spoon, and with a steady hand emptied it into the bottle. She took six spoonfuls to make sure. By the time it was safely corked and in Myrtle's pocket, the heady smell was making Rosemary giddy. She pulled herself together and replaced the glass stopper in the huge bottle. Then she climbed a little unsteadily down the ladder and went into the dispensary to wash her hands.

'It'll be a new assistant instead of me next week as well, if Mr Fudge finds out about this!' said Myrtle worriedly.

'He won't,' said Rosemary. 'If you can give Albert a dose this afternoon he can start work again tomorrow! I must run now, I'm going to be terribly late for dinner!'

26

Council of War

WHEN Rosemary reached home, she was just in time to take John's dinner in to him on a tray.

'It's chops and peas and new potatoes!' she said as she removed the cover.

'Good!' said John. 'Have you got the cold cure?'

Rosemary nodded and told him about Mrs Cantrip and the green mixture. The idea of Rosemary as the old woman's apprentice he seemed to think very funny.

'But I've got some news for you, too. The attack will be in two days' time!'

'How do you know?'

'Mr Featherstone came in to see me. He's staying to lunch. He had seen it announced in the local paper. He said that instead of the two towns being ashamed of a disgraceful piece of ribbon development, they were actually going to celebrate its being finished with what the newspaper called a Friendship Ceremony.'

'What's ribbon development?' asked Rosemary.

'He said it was building a lot of houses along the roadside without proper planning. Anyway, there's to be music and speechifying, and he said would we all like to come and see it. Then your mother could celebrate finishing the Julius Caesar clothes.'

'What did Mummy say?'

'She laughed and said, "What nonsense," and that she liked making the acting clothes anyway. But she looked pleased, and it's all settled. We must let Blanda-mour know as soon as possible.'

'She's coming this afternoon,' said Rosemary. 'To see the kittens and say thank you to us. I met Woppit as I was coming home. We had better have a council of war up here.'

It was three o'clock before Blandamour arrived. She was followed by Merbeck and Woppit, and to their surprise Tudge came trotting behind at a respectful distance. He had called to see his sister.

Rosemary had brushed the protesting kittens until their coats gleamed. Calidor's white socks were spotless. Every whisker was in order. They both sat on John's bed rehearsing the Kitten's Welcome to His Parents which all well-bred animals use. It begins:

> *Accept my warm, respectful purr,*
> *Clean, my paws, and trim, my fur.*

But when their mother walked through the open door they got no further than 'Accept my warm ...' before they scrambled off the bed and ran helter-skelter to her. They rubbed themselves against her snow-white sides, mingling their shrill, quick purrs with her deeper, steadier hum,.

'My children! My little children!' said Blanda-mour as she licked their upturned faces. Both Calidor and Pergamond were telling their adventures at the same time, in shrill, excited voices. 'Hush! hush, my dears. Later,' said their mother and turned to John and Rosemary.

'I have no words with which to thank you for all you have done!' she began.

'That's all right, your Majesty,' said John awk-wardly. 'Don't bother. Besides, we haven't really got time. The attack will be in two days. We've just heard!'

While he told her what he knew, Blandamour leapt on to the bed, closely followed by her Councillor. The kittens scrambled up the bedspread and began jostling for the place nearest their mother, until she silenced them with a scoop of her paw. There was a scuffle as Tudge tried to leap up, too. Woppit's voice could be heard coming from under the bed, making such remarks as 'Like your impudence!' and 'The likes of us.' At last they all listened to John in silence. He told them of the activity among the Broomhurst cats that he had seen from the back of the lorry, and the conversation he and Rosemary had overheard near Adelaide Row. At last Merbeck spoke.

'Some of this we knew already. What we did not know was when the last little gap in the wall would be finished and the Cat Causeway completed. That is the news we have been waiting for. Now, we can act!'

'Two days doesn't seem very long to get ready when the others have been stirring up their followers for weeks!' said Rosemary anxiously.

'Do not worry. We have not been idle,' said Blandamour. 'Contented, well-governed cats do not need to be brought to heel with bribery and fiery speeches.'

'We have two advantages,' said Merbeck. 'First, Grisana does not know that we are warned and well-prepared; secondly, they will have only one road of approach, the newly finished garden walls of Broomhurst Road.'

'But how do you know that they won't come pouring across the fields on either side?' said Rosemary.

Merbeck turned his grizzled face toward her. 'Because if cats begin fighting on human ground, then humans will join in, and when that happens, in their blundering way they set about every cat in sight, with brooms and buckets of water and even hose pipes. I've seen it happen. How are they to know which cats are which?'

Tudge's voice from under the bed was heard to mutter, 'Daft creatures, humans!' to be hastily shushed by Woppit.

'Cat troubles must be decided in cat country, and beyond a scuffle or two the humans will know nothing about it,' went on Merbeck. 'Now, as I see it, the enemy, not knowing that we shall be alert and watching every movement, at a given signal will pour into Fallowhithe.'

'And you will fall silently on them as they arrive along the causeway and finish 'em off!' said John bouncing up and down in bed. 'Easy!'

'Not so easy!' went on Merbeck. 'Already many enemy cats have slipped into the town – lawless, insolent creatures, urged on by their wicked Queen. Provided that they still think themselves unnoticed, it seems to us that there will be some prearranged meeting place where they will plan to meet the newcomers. The main body of animals, who will come pouring along the Causeway, must at all costs be stopped from joining the others at this meeting place. Where that will be it is for us to find out.'

The hair on the ridge of the old cat's back was bristling, and his tail was lashing fiercely from side to side.

'Will you have enough cats to turn them back?' asked Rosemary anxiously.

'We are a highly organized society, my dear young lady!' said Merbeck. 'Every road, square and terrace has its cat guardian. They have had their instructions for some days. Every ten houses has at least six able-bodied animals who would fight to the last claw, cat and kitten, for their Queen, and their families. "The choice of the best hearthrugs for Broomhurst animals" indeed!'

'But what about Mrs Cantrip and Miss Dibdin?' asked Rosemary. 'Aren't you forgetting them?'

'I don't think we need bother about Miss Dibdin,' said John. 'She wasn't much good anyway, but without her book of spells she can't even try to do anything. As for Mrs Cantrip, you said yourself, Rosie, that she had practically nothing left in her magic cupboard.'

'There were only two things left, a little bit of Flying Philtre in a tin, but Miss Dibdin said she had finished that on the broom, and a pinch of brownish powder in a pickle jar, but I can't remember what it said on the label, M-i-n . . . something.'

'Well, whatever it was, I shouldn't think she could do much damage with a few grains.'

Rosemary frowned. 'I wonder what she meant when she said she'd still got a shot in her locker then? She kept her word to Grisana about the kittens, and she may still try to "kidnap" Queen Blandamour.'

'You talk as though I am as feeble as a kitten with its eyes closed!' said Blandamour. 'I can defend myself!' she added proudly.

'I hope that will not be necessary,' said Merbeck. 'From now on you shall be guarded night and day!'

'Don't you think –' began Rosemary uneasily.

'I think you're fussing!' said John.

'I will be careful,' said Blandamour, 'I promise you that.'

'And speaking of the royal kittens!' went on Merbeck thoughtfully, 'it seems to me that while they are here they may still be in danger. Would it not be better to hide them?'

'But where?'

Promptly from under the bed came the voice of Tudge. 'At Turley's Farm for sure! Oh, leave me be, Woppit, you old busybody!' he added in a hoarse whisper.

'Come here, my faithful Tudge!' said Blandamour.

Tudge heaved his ungainly form onto the bed, ducked awkwardly but respectfully at the white cat and said, 'If you'll pardon the liberty, not never before having even passed the time of day with royalty, but willing to serve you, ma'am, and them royal kits to the last whisker.' He took a deep breath. 'Now I was thinking, at Turley's cats and kittens is as common as pebbles on a gravel path, and if so be I was to say my sister Woppit was come from the town with her two kitlings for a holiday, nobody wouldn't think twice about it, if so be your Majesty wouldn't take it as a liberty ...' his voice trailed off.

'My good Tudge, it is an excellent idea. With you and Woppit to guard them, I am sure they will come to no harm.'

'But I want to defend Father's kingdom, too!' complained Calidor. 'I'd give it 'em!' He pounced violently on John's toes which John had moved unwarily under the bedclothes. Pergamond did not seem pleased at this arrangement either.

'Nasty, common, country cats!' she complained with a toss of her tortoise-shell head.

Blandamour for once looked really angry and she gave her a cuff that sent her rolling. But the farm cat did not seem offended.

'Common and country maybe, little royal ma'am, but nasty, no! Now come along with old Tudge, and perhaps he'll tell you about some of the adventures he had when he were at sea aboard the *Mary Jane*.'

Calidor struggled down the trailing bedspread onto the floor. 'Were you really at sea?' he said.

'Ship's cat, I were,' said Tudge. 'Together with my mate Wyb. High old times we had, what with the flying fish.'

'Flying fish?' said Pergamond, and scrambled down, too.

'Ah, my pretty, like sardines with wings, but not so tasty. Now, there was one night when a storm blew up . . .'

The two kittens trotted off, one on either side of Tudge, listening eagerly. Before he went through the door, he turned and winked broadly.

Woppit tossed her head and bowed at the same time, hoping that this would show both respect for Queen Blandamour and disapproval of her brother's low manners. Then she followed the kittens.

'I suppose we couldn't help when the attack comes?' asked John.

Blandamour shook her head. 'That would be very unwise. Grisana cheated by enrolling the help of Mrs Cantrip. You have done for us what we could never have done alone. If they must quarrel, cats against cats and humans against humans, that is the order of things.'

'If we can arrange for you to be present we will send a message,' said Merbeck. 'But now we must go. There is so much to do!'

27

The Friendship Ceremony

MRS BROWN kept John in bed all the next day, but before breakfast on Friday, Rosemary went to fetch the milk. She ran quickly downstairs, and as she picked up the two bottles the milkman had left for Mrs Brown, a young cat with a glossy black coat and a white face trotted briskly up to her.

'Name of Rosemary?' he asked.

'Yes, that's me.'

'Message for you from Councillor Merbeck,' he said importantly. Then he looked around cautiously and lowered his voice. 'The attack is planned for midnight tonight. Be the at Green Cave at half-past eleven.'

'Yes, but ...' began Rosemary.

'Can't stop, too much to do!' said the black cat and hurried away.

'Good oh!' said John when she told him. He was dressed and making the toast for breakfast in front of the gas fire in the sitting room. 'I hoped they wouldn't forget us. I do want to be in on the attack.'

'I don't think I want to be there much,' said Rosemary. 'But on the other hand I should be miserable at home not knowing what was happening.'

'Anyway, we've got this Friendship affair this afternoon,' said John.

It was due to begin at half past two. At two o'clock, after a very merry lunch, for Mr Featherstone had joined them again, John carried down the picnic basket. They were going to make an outing of it.

'Why, Mummy!' said Rosemary, as her mother got into Mr Featherstone's ancient car, 'what a lovely new dress!'

'I think you look gorgeous!' said John.

'I couldn't put it better myself,' said Mr Featherstone gravely. 'Gorgeous is the word!'

Mrs Brown went quite pink, but she laughed and said she was sure it was time they started.

When they reached the new houses of Broomhurst Road, there was no doubt where the ceremony was to be held. A long row of cars was parked on either side, and a loud speaker van was playing 'Land of Hope and Glory'. The completed houses stretched in an unbroken line. Nearly all of them had curtains at the windows, and the corner where John had hidden from Mrs Cantrip behind the half-built wall already housed a washing machine.

A crowd had collected round the one unfinished part, a short stretch of garden wall. Behind it stood the Mayors of Broomhurst and Fallowhithe in their mayoral robes, supported by a number of important local people. When the loud speaker had finished playing, the Mayor of Fallowhithe made a long speech about what an historic occasion it was for both towns and one which he hoped would bind them more firmly together in a bond of friendship and healthy rivalry. Then the Major of Broomhurst replied in much the same way. The speeches were rather long, and John, whose attention was wandering, suddenly nudged Rosemary.

'Look! Over there in the front row!'

It was Mrs Cantrip. She was listening very solemnly and clapping from time to time rather more loudly than was necessary. At last the speeches were over and the Mayor of each town took a trowel and some mortar, and amidst some laughter, laid two bricks side by side in token of the cementing of the friendship between Broomhurst and Fallowhithe, and Mrs Cantrip clapped so loudly that people turned and stared.

'Who is that extraordinary old woman?' asked Mr Featherstone. Both John and Rosemary thought it better not to tell him. Then the Mayors shook hands and the loud speaker van played 'Jerusalem', followed by 'God Save the Queen', and the crowds began to move away.

'There's nothing more to wait for,' said Mrs Brown.

'Let's wait a bit longer,' said Rosemary, who felt unwilling to go.

'There's nothing more to see,' said Mr Featherstone, 'except the man who is finishing the wall.'

A bricklayer was skillfully and rapidly filling up the rest of the gap. Rosemary thought it was the same man to whom they had talked on the day they had found the rocking chair. Thinking of the rocking chair reminded her of Mrs Cantrip. She looked around, but the old woman was gone.

'Just look at those two cats!' said Mrs Brown.

They were sitting behind the workman, apparently half asleep, their eyes nearly closed. But there was an alertness about them that did not deceive Rosemary.

'They look like Noggin and Swabber, those two cats we met on the high place!' she whispered to John.

'Will you finish the wall today?' asked Mrs Brown.

'Bless you, yes!' said the man, skillfully scraping off a piece of unwanted mortar and slapping it into position.

The cats were wide awake now. They were staring at the bricklayer with unblinking eyes.

'By five o'clock this afternoon it'll all be done, and smooth on the top as your Ma's tape measure!' he said to Rosemary, and at the word 'five', Noggin and Swabber were off down the road to Broomhurst like greased lightning, as John put it.

'And talking of lightning, I think there's thunder about,' said Mr Featherstone.

It was certainly very close. 'I vote we have tea in Bagshott Wood. It may be cooler there.'

The tea was delicious, with ice cream and some late raspberries brought by Mr Featherstone as his share of the feast. Afterwards, John and Rosemary lay on their backs in the dry beech leaves, and looked up at the shifting chinks of sky between the branches above them. They had so much to think about that they were rather quiet. The grownups talked earnestly together, but the children lay there listening to the animal conversations going on around them.

A bird sang a song somewhere about the joys of bringing up a family. The song had a chorus of trills and tralas, and the last verse went on to say that perhaps the joy of being free again when the family had flown away was even better. Two spiders were arguing about the best way to start a web between two trees. A rabbit looked around a stump and said in disgust, 'More humans!' and disappeared again.

Mrs Brown and Mr Featherstone went off for a walk, and as the flowered dress and the grey flannels disappeared between the trees, Rosemary said, 'You know, the best part of all this magic has been the power to hear animals talk. I don't think I could bear to have it taken away now!'

'Nor me,' said John. 'You know, I think waiting is the hardest thing of all to do. I don't think half past eleven tonight will ever come!'

28

The Attack

IN spite of their doubt, half past eleven did come at last. Mrs Brown had gone to bed early.

'That long walk with Mr Featherstone this afternoon must have made her tired,' whispered John as they crept downstairs with their sandals in their hands. This time they were taking no chances and were fully dressed.

It was hot and very still in the darkened garden. In the Green Cave, not a leaf stirred above them. They took it in turns to sit on the biscuit tin to put on their sandals. Presently a darker shadow slipped between the bushes, and the brisk voice of the cat who had delivered the message that morning said, 'Greetings to you, sir and miss!'

'Greetings to you!' said Rosemary politely.

'I have been instructed to see you safely to headquarters, and I assure you, you will be perfectly safe in my charge.'

'That's very good of you,' said John, who felt quite capable of looking after himself and Rosemary. 'But all the same –'

'Not at all!' broke in the animal, as they crawled out of the Green Cave. 'Not that it is for everybody I'd risk missing my place in the battle, no sir! But your fame has gone far and wide, as the gallant rescuers of the royal kittens, and I'd look on it as an honour,' he said graciously. 'Leadbitter is the name.'

They followed him out of the garden into the road.

'Where are the headquarters?' asked Rosemary.

'Ssh!' said Leadbitter hurriedly. 'The very lamp-posts may have ears!' he whispered. 'Follow me!'

John and Rosemary followed. Leadbitter trotted on in the swift, effortless way of the cat with a purpose, and they had their work cut out to keep up with him. An occasional car sped by, and sometimes a late home-comer walked quickly past, and looked curiously at the two children. Several times they were overtaken by other cats hurrying in the same direction. To each one Leadbitter called softly, 'Bittem?' and the animal would answer, 'Haddock heads!' And apparently satisfied, Leadbitter would trot on again. Once they saw a large tabby cat accompanied by a very small one. 'This is not a night for kittens to be abroad, ma'am!' said Leadbitter firmly. 'Better take him indoors as quickly as possible!'

'Yes, sir, this very minute, sir. I'm taking him out of harm's way to his auntie, sir!' came the answer.

They hurried on, and as they neared the Old Town, John said, 'Rosie, look at that wall!'

The pavement along which they were hurrying ran beside a wall which towered like a cliff above them. Rosemary looked up and saw along the top a steady stream of animals, trotting silently, purposefully. Leadbitter turned to see why they had stopped, and looked up, too.

'Ours,' he said briefly. 'Come on!'

When at last they turned the corner at the end of the street, they found themselves by a churchyard.

'St Michael's!' said Rosemary.

'It's a ruin, isn't it?' asked John.

Rosemary nodded.

'Only since the war. The tower is complete, though.

People pay sixpence to go up and see the view from the top through the telescope. Is that where the headquarters are?' she asked. 'But how can we get inside? The keeper locks it every night.'

'Well, tonight isn't the first time he's forgotten!' said Leadbitter, and trotted across the road and up to the iron studded door. 'Go on! Open it! We have other means of getting to the top, but you will have to use the stairs.'

John turned the handle. The door opened easily. It was dark inside the tower, but as their eyes grew accustomed to the gloom, they saw a winding stair up which they followed their guide, who was, of course, able to see perfectly well. As they stumbled up behind him, they passed three narrow windows, by which they paused to regain their breath. Through the first they saw they were level with the second floor windows of the houses opposite. Through the second window they were level with the roof tops. But when they plodded rather breathlessly past the third window, they could see nothing but the deep blue of the night sky. At last they reached the belfry where the three church bells hung, silent, above them. Rosemary put up her arm as something swooped and fluttered around their heads. It was a bat.

'A disgraceful intrusion!' it complained in a high, peevish voice. 'Bats in the belfry I always understood it was, not dozens of cats, and now two great lumbering humans as well!'

'I'm so sorry,' said Rosemary. 'We didn't mean to disturb you, and we will try not to lumber.'

'Hearing humans, eh?' twittered the bat. 'Well, I suppose that's different,' and he darted through the open trap door above them.

Leadbitter, followed by John and Rosemary, climbed up the wooden ladder that led to the square of star-studded sky. He paused as a cat's head was outlined against the stars, and a pair of green eyes looked down on them. 'Halt, and give the password!' said the head.

'Haddock heads!' said Leadbitter. 'I've brought the sir and miss.'

'The Councillor is waiting for you. Look lively and come up.'

They came out into the night air. Many times Rosemary had paid her sixpence and climbed the tall church tower to look through the telescope which stood at the top. You could see the roofs of Fallowhithe spread beneath. Away in the distance to the south, across the fields, you could see the smudge of houses that was Broomhurst. But that, of course, was in daylight. With John she came out, not onto the leaded roof she had expected, but onto an uneven rocky hollow, surrounded, not by the carved pinnacles of the church tower, but by strangely formed jagged rocks. There was no telescope. Where Rosemary thought it stood was a little, stunted tree. But they had no time to examine anything as Merbeck trotted up.

'My dear John and Rosemary, you are just in time! From here you will be able to watch the progress of the attack in safety. What are you fidgeting for, Leadbitter? Yes, yes, of course you may go now!'

Leadbitter gave a quick bow to Rosemary.

'Good luck, my boy!' called Merbeck. 'For Queen and country! I only wish I were ten years younger!' But Leadbitter had already disappeared.

'But where is Queen Blandamour?' asked John.

'She insisted on addressing our faithful Fallowhithe animals before the attack.'

'Like Queen Elizabeth the First at Tilbury before the Spanish Armada,' whispered Rosemary.

'She is surrounded by a powerful bodyguard, and already she should be on her way back here. But come and see.'

He led them to the rocky parapet where several cats, who were gazing down, made room for them. From their dizzy pinnacle of rock they could see Fallowhithe spread out beneath, but just as the roof of the high place had seemed not a roof but a grassy plateau, so it seemed in the clear starlit night that they were looking down, not on the roofs and chimneys of a town, but on a mountainous, craggy country, scored with valleys and canyons. It stretched away to the north till it was lost in the darkness. To the south, a low range of hills narrowed to what looked like a spur of land, which dwindled in its turn into a ribbon which pointed straight as a ruler into the darkness where they knew Broomhurst must be.

'Is that the Causeway?' asked John.

Merbeck nodded.

There was a low mist over the fields on either side which might well have been the sea.

'It all looks so peaceful!' said Rosemary.

'Maybe,' said Merbeck. 'But wait until the clocks strike midnight! My spies discovered that that is when the attack is planned. Do you remember the old skating rink?'

Rosemary nodded. She remembered the rink as a low building enclosed by a jumble of tall shops and offices. The Councillor waved with his paw toward a low lying hollow surrounded by rocky hills.

'That is one of the places where the Broomhurst cats plan to gather, when they have crept in secretly by the Causeway, and there they expect to be joined by their friends who have already wormed their way into the town. There is a second meeting place to the north on Fire Station Heights.'

'But I can't see any cats!' said John.

'There is nothing so still as a cat that does not wish to be seen,' said Merbeck. 'Wait!'

As he spoke, behind them the Cathedral clock struck twelve, with its deep, booming voice, to be joined by the quick eager chimes of the clock of the Market Hall. Hard on its heels came the station clock, and like distant echoes sounded the clocks of St Anne's Church and Fallowhithe High School. When there was nothing left of the chimes but a faint vibration in the air, Merbeck said, 'Now look at Skating Rink Hollow!'

'Something's moving!' said John.

'The enemy!' said Merbeck.

It was as though the surface of the hollow was a giant cauldron, and someone was stirring it with a huge wooden spoon. Little eddies of cats ran up the surrounding slopes and joined the ones already there.

'Hm,' said Merbeck, 'there were more of them already here than I imagined.'

He turned toward the Causeway. It was as though in the dark, out of sight, a bottle of ink had been spilled along its width, and had seeped along the top toward Fallowhithe.

'Broomhurst cats,' said Merbeck briefly.

'Two hundred strong they must be!' said one of the animals standing at Merbeck's side.

'Oh dear, can't we do something?' said Rosemary anxiously. 'Before it's too late!'

'Have patience. Remember they do not know we have been warned!' said Merbeck.

The Causeway cats had nearly reached the walls, or hills, of Fallowhithe. 'Give the signal,' he said sharply. 'Now!'

The cat beside him threw back his head and gave a low bubbling cry which rose in the air, growing shrill and clear till it split the silence like a bugle call. Far away came an answering cry, then from different parts of the town, another and another.

'You see we are not unprepared! That was the signal for the defenders to advance!' said Merbeck. 'Now watch. Their orders are to stop the animals on the Causeway from joining their friends on Skating Rink Hollow and Fire Station Heights, both of which are surrounded by picked Fallowhithe cats.'

Something was happening on the Causeway. At the sound of the bugle call the oncoming army of Broomhurst cats halted, then they moved on again more slowly. They kept closely together, but finding themselves unhindered, quickened their pace until they reached the slopes that were the first roof tops of Fallowhithe, and as they spread out and moved up the incline, the slope on the other side seemed to come alive and move up to meet them. It was the Fallowhithe cats who had been waiting, so still and silent that they had seemed part of the landscape itself. With bloodcurdling cries they surged up to the top and hurled themselves on the enemy, spitting their defiance.

From the lookout John and Rosemary could see the struggling mass swaying first one way and then another.

'But we can't tell what's happening!' said Rosemary in distress.

'I think all is going well!' said Merbeck. 'We shall

know more when the dispatches start coming in. I wish Her Majesty were here to watch. It is high time she returned,' he said uneasily.

But John and Rosemary were looking towards Skating Rink Hollow. This was farther away, so that they could not see so clearly what was going on. But whereas it had looked like a cauldron stirred with a spoon when the enemy cats first began to move, it now looked as though the cauldron was boiling furiously, as more and more Fallowhithe animals hurled themselves into the hollow. From time to time a rallying cry would break the silence of the night with its shrill eerie note, while small skirmishes broke out all over the town as the Broomhurst animals scattered, spitting and swearing.

The clocks chimed the quarter, and the half hour, and a messenger cat came panting up to Merbeck.

'The Causeway fight is going well, sir. A number of the enemy have turned tail!'

'The Fire Station Heights affair is satisfactory, sir!' said another cat breathlessly. 'But there is trouble at Skating Rink Hollow. We're outnumbered!'

'Bring up some of the reserves,' snapped Merbeck. 'Better use the Garbage Foragers – scum of the town, but mangificent fighters!' he added for John's benefit. 'Why does not Her Majesty come?'

'Councillor! Sir!' said a voice. 'It's Leadbitter! He's wounded.'

They turned. Leadbitter stood panting behind them. One ear was torn, and there was a gash in his side.

'Terrible news!' he said. 'The Queen! She's gone!'

29

Minuscule Magic

'The Queen gone?' repeated Merbeck. 'When? How did it happen?'

'She was returning after her speech. Things were getting pretty hot, and the Captain of the Queen's Guard enrolled a few cats who were passing – in case of trouble – and I was one. Well, we were in a solid ring around her, nose to tail, and one minute she was there . . . and the next . . . she was nowhere to be seen!'

'Does anyone else know this besides the bodyguard?' asked Merbeck anxiously.

'I'm afraid they do. The Captain called to every cat in Fairfax Market to search.'

'Fairfax Market!' said John and Rosemary together.

'Can you tell us exactly where it happened?' asked John.

'We were in Cat Country. We'd jumped down to the pavement to avoid a skirmish between half a dozen animals, and we were keeping well into the wall, when a window opened just above. A human looked out and laughed, not a nice noise it wasn't, and then . . . the Queen was gone!'

'Her white coat must have shown up as clearly as spilt milk,' said Merbeck.

'Quick,' said John. 'Can you remember anything about the house you were near?'

'Not much,' said Leadbitter. 'I was too busy. Hold on though! There was a door that opened and closed very quickly while we were searching. I looked around when I heard a bang, and it was scarlet half way down.'

'Mrs Cantrip!' said Rosemary.

John nodded grimly.

Another messenger came up.

'Sir Councillor, things are going against us! A fresh wave of the enemy has stormed the Causeway, and Fallowhithe cats are falling back. They've heard the Queen has disappeared, and it's shaken 'em badly!'

'Come on, Rosie!' said John. 'It looks as though we may be able to help after all.' He turned to Merbeck. 'If Mrs Cantrip has got her, we'll get her back, somehow!'

'Of course we will!' said Rosemary stoutly. 'Come on, John!'

'Hurry!' said Merbeck. 'There is no time to lose!'

Together they scrambled down the rocky chasm, which they knew led to the belfry. Once their feet were on the wooden ladder the shadowy cat world disappeared, and although they neither of them stopped to say so, it was a relief to feel the solid firmness of the winding stairs, even though they had to feel their way down in the dark. The bank of cloud had mounted higher in the sky, and as they ran through the churchyard, there was a low rumble of distant thunder. They did not stop to look up at the swaying battle on the roofs of the houses opposite, but ran as fast as they could to Fairfax Market. Without stopping to think what they would do next, they hammered on the scarlet front door of Mrs Cantrip's house.

It opened quickly.

'It's you, is it? I thought as much, for all your talk of backing out,' said the old woman accusingly to Rosemary.

Rosemary had no time to point out that she had never talked about it at all, before John demanded fiercely. 'Queen Blandamour! Where is she? You've got her hidden somewhere!'

'If you're so certain, you'd best come in and see for yourselves!' said Mrs Cantrip, with a mocking curtsy.

They followed the old woman through the bare room inside the front door, which had nowhere to hide a fly, let alone a well-grown, white cat, and into the little kitchen beyond.

'Where is she?' repeated John.

Mrs Cantrip sat herself down in the rocking chair and began to rock herself to and fro.

'If seeing's believing, and you can't see her, well, it proves she isn't here, young man. So look as much as you've a mind to. Then perhaps you'll leave a law-abiding old woman to her night's rest.'

John and Rosemary stood in the middle of the floor. By the flickering light of a candle in a bottle they looked around. It was very quiet in the little room. There was no sound except the rhythmical rocking of the chair on the tiled floor. An occasional scuffle outside was the only sign of the battle that was raging above them. There was nothing behind the cloak that hung on a peg on the door. Their hopes were raised by a tall thin cupboard by the fireplace, but when they looked inside there was nothing but Miss Dibdin's flying broom, and an ordinary sweeping broom very upright in a corner, as though it did not much care for the other's company. Mrs Cantrip chuckled at their disappointment.

On the table in the middle of the room were the remains of a meal. It was laid for two. John noticed that one plate and the cup and saucer beside it were empty, but the other had some cold meat and pickles on it, and only half of the cup of tea had been drunk, as though someone had left the table in a hurry.

'Where is Miss Dibdin?' asked Rosemary.

'How should I know?' said Mrs Cantrip, with her head on one side. 'With your precious white cat, for all I know.'

'Go and look upstairs, Rosie!' said John.

Rosemary went, and while she was gone, Mrs Cantrip went on rocking and looking at John with a twisted smile. He began to wonder if they had made a mistake after all. Rosemary came down again and reported that there was no sign of Miss Dibdin and no trace of Blandamour. She had looked in every drawer and cupboard and corner.

'I've had enough of your busybodying,' said Mrs Cantrip. 'I'm going to sleep.'

She took a large handkerchief out of her pocket, spread it over her face and linked her hands over her waist. But the vigorous rocking of the chair suggested someone very wide awake indeed.

'If only we could see better. It's so dark!' said John.

'I believe she keeps her candles in here,' said Rosemary, and she went to the little hanging cupboard behind the door.

'Top shelf, left-hand side,' said Mrs Cantrip from under the handkerchief. John and Rosemary looked at each other in a puzzled way. They had never known Mrs Cantrip to be obliging before, and the very strangeness of it made them suspicious.

'Light as many of 'em as you like,' said the old woman. Rosemary took down three candles.

'There's a box of matches here,' she said and picked it up from the bottom shelf. But Mrs Cantrip whipped the handkerchief from her face and said fiercely, 'Don't you touch it! Put it down!'

Now you will have noticed that everyone who picks up a box of matches gives it a little shake to see if there are any matches inside. Rosemary obediently put the box down, but she noticed that although it was not light enough to be empty, it did not make the little rattle that matches usually do. It had been lying on the bottom shelf of the cupboard where she remembered Mrs Cantrip had kept the few little bits of magic she had left. Only the glass pickle jar was there, but now it was empty, too. The label on it said MINUSCULE MAGIC.

'Minuscule!' said John. 'I've seen that word somewhere, I wish I could think –'

'I shouldn't bother, dear!' said Mrs Cantrip. 'You light the pretty candles from the one in the bottle. It's a pity to waste good matches!' She was smiling once more.

John lit the candles and stuck them in a row on the mantelpiece, and as he lit the third one he suddenly said, 'I've got it! We were playing that spelling game, and Daddy used it, and we all said there wasn't such a word as minuscule, and Daddy said there was and it meant very, very tiny!'

Mrs Cantrip jumped up from her chair so violently that she knocked it over backwards. For a few seconds one could have heard a pin drop, and then from behind Rosemary, who was still standing in front of the open cupboard, came a faint, faint scrabbling noise together with a tiny shrill 'meow'. At first she thought it was a mouse, but, as everybody knows, mice don't mew.

'The matchbox!' she said.

Mrs Cantrip strode across the room, but Rosemary was too quick for her. She picked it up and gently slid it open. Fitting neatly, curled up inside, was a tiny, tiny white cat!

'It's Blandamour! You've made her small with the Minuscule Magic!' said Rosemary.

30

The Return of the Kings

John and Rosemary peered at the minute white cat.

'Oh, Blandamour, I'm so thankful we've found you!' whispered Rosemary.

The tiny creature rubbed against her outstretched forefinger, and purred with a sound no louder than the ticking of the smallest watch.

'Well, what are you going to do about it?' asked Mrs Cantrip defiantly. 'Say to them Fallowhithe animals, "Here's your Queen back again. I'm sorry she's no bigger than a ginger biscuit?" Do you think they'll believe you? Well you needn't bother, I shouldn't think it matters much by now. Not that I care two pennyworth of pentagons who wins, the Fallowhithe cats or the Broomhurst ones. And it's no use asking for the counter-spell,' she went on fiercely. 'I've done enough obliging of you for one night and I'm doing no more. Three candle ends I've given you, and that's generous.'

'Perhaps Miss Dibdin would help us,' suggested Rosemary.

'Yes, where is she?' asked John, looking at the unfinished meal on the table.

'Where she won't be no help to you!' snapped Mrs Cantrip.

'What have you done to her?' asked John sharply.

'She shouldn't have been so aggravating,' said the old woman sullenly. 'Serves her right!'

'Miss Dibdin, where are you?' called Rosemary anxiously.

As if in answer a small round object rolled off the top shelf of the cupboard behind her and fell with a plop on to the floor. It was a nutmeg. They looked at the top shelf, and struggling to push its way between a bag of sugar and a packet of rice was a tiny, doll-like figure, in a neat tweed jacket and shirt.

'Miss Dibdin!' said John.

'How could you?' said Rosemary accusingly to Mrs Cantrip.

The old woman tossed her head, but she seemed anxious not to look Rosemary in the eye.

'Well, I had to keep her out of mischief somehow,' she said sullenly. 'I couldn't have her messing up my last crumb of magic with her silly ways.'

'When did you do it?' asked John.

'It suddenly came over me in the middle of supper, so I blew a grain or two of Minuscule Magic on her just as she helped herself to pickles, and popped her in the cupboard in a potted meat jar to keep her safe. I can't think how she got out. You can have her if you want to, she's no use to me. And the cat, too, for that matter. The battle is over by now, I shouldn't wonder.'

'The battle!' said Rosemary. 'I'd almost forgotten all about it.'

As if to remind them, there was a prolonged scuffle outside and far away a sharp cat call.

'Come on, Rosie, let's get back to headquarters. I'll put Miss Dibdin in my pocket, and you take Blandamour.'

Very gently he picked up Miss Dibdin between his finger and thumb. She had been sitting in a dazed way on a pepper pot. He popped her back into the potted meat jar and put it in the top pocket of his blazer. Rosemary picked up the matchbox, and when the tiny cat had curled herself up inside, closed it softly. Together they hurried out into Fairfax Market. There they looked up anxiously at the roofs above them, expecting to see the struggling shapes that had swayed and fought there when they had made their way to Mrs Cantrip's house. But there seemed nothing to be seen but deserted walls and roofs, and the sounds of battle sounded faint and far away. A solitary cat limped past them. 'Bitten!' called John softly.

'What's happening?' asked Rosemary. 'Has the Fallowhithe army won?'

'Won!' said the cat bitterly. 'It won't be long now before the Broomhurst creatures are in full control. They have swept over half the town. Already this is enemy-held territory. There are pockets of our animals here and there, harrying where they get the chance, but our fellows are retreating to the other end of the town.'

'Oh dear!' said Rosemary.

'Are the headquarters on the church tower still?' asked John.

'Bless you, no! The last time I saw Councillor Merbeck, he was defending Swimming Bath Slopes. He'd been joined by a company of fierce farm cats – terrible fighters they are. They call themselves Turley's Terrors. But I can't stop gossiping here. I'm carrying dispatches.'

'Come on, Rosie, let's make for the Swimming Bath. Follow me!' said John. 'I think I know the way.'

'Good luck to you, hearing humans!' the cat called after them.

They ran up Green Man Lane, down Pottery Court,

across the High Street where the traffic lights winked busily to an empty road. Then, cutting down Ponsonby Street, they turned into Bath Road. At first they came across an occasional tussling pair of cats above them, and then groups and companies, until, when they reached the swimming baths, the roof was a solid mass of struggling animals. A haze of flying fur made it difficult to see what was happening.

'How can we get up there?' said Rosemary anxiously.

'Quick, the garages at the end!' said John.

They dashed to the back of the building where a row of garages in a cobbled yard were built against the end wall of the swimming baths. Outside one of the garages, a lorry was parked, loaded with something under a tarpaulin which rose to within a few feet of the garage roof. They clambered on to the bonnet of the lorry, and from there to the roof. They scrambled over the tarpaulin, slipping and sliding on its uneven surface.

'Here, I'll give you a leg up on to the roof!' said John.

An urgent, eerie cat call rose over the hissing and spitting just above them. Rosemary's courage wavered for a moment, but she gritted her teeth and climbed on to John's bowed back. From there she could easily reach the garage roof. She pulled herself up, the soft grass of Cat Country saving her from grazed knees and torn hands. Then, lying on her stomach, she stretched down to help John up after her.

They were on a narrow ledge with a high bank sloping steeply in front of them. Cautiously they scrambled up till they could see over the top. The bank of clouds that had lain on the horizon in a tumbled heap earlier in the evening had mounted and grown, until only

here and there a gap showed serenely shining stars. It had become oppressively hot, and the spit and hiss of fighting cats was lost from time to time in the grumble of distant thunder. Dimly they could see below them a drop of several feet. Then the ground sloped gently away, but whether the surface was of grass or rock they could not see, for the whole surface heaved and tossed like a stormy sea, a sea not of waves but of fighting cats, and the air was full of strange, throaty cat taunts.

Suddenly, there was a very loud rumble of thunder followed by a flash of lightning. For one flickering

second the whole scene was lit up, and just below them with his back against the little cliff was an old, old cat with a very small black animal beside him. Together they were warding off a huge, grinning sandy tom.

'Merbeck!' called John. 'Calidor! It's us, John and Rosemary.'

'Greetings!' panted Merbeck. 'We can't hold out much longer. This is our last stand!'

A second shape took its place beside Merbeck just as the sandy cat made a vicious lunge at Calidor, and another flash of lightning showed Tudge laying about him like a windmill, and the sandy cat slinking away.

'To me, Turleys!' he called. 'Us'll go down fighting!' From the mass of shifting shapes, here and there one would shake itself clear and force its way to where Tudge and Merbeck and little Calidor stood with their backs against the cliff.

John was banging the palm of one hand with his other fist. 'Go it! Oh, go it, Tudge and Merbeck!'

'And go it me, too!' came in an excited squeak from Calidor.

So absorbed was John that he did not notice Rosemary tugging at his jacket and calling him anxiously.

'John, John, you must listen!'

'What's the matter?' he said impatiently.

'Some more cats, a whole company of them, coming towards us along the ridge. I saw them in that last flash of lightning!'

'More cats?' said John grimly. 'Then I should think that just about finishes it. Merbeck!' he called through his curved hands. 'There's another company moving up behind you!'

'This . . . is . . . the . . . end!' panted the Councillor.

In the added gloom that seemed to follow each flash, Rosemary saw that the dark shape of the approaching animals was nearly upon them.

'They're here, Merbeck!' she called desperately. 'I can see them!'

Merbeck gave a gallant, despairing cry of, 'Who goes there?'

The answer came back clear and strong, 'I, Carbonel!' And in a double flash of lightning they saw him standing on the high bank. His magnificent head was raised inquiringly, while behind stood a splendid company of animals. For a second they were lit up so clearly that John and Rosemary saw behind him a lean, blue-eyed cat from Siam, a thin, big-boned cat from Egypt, a long-haired Persian cat, cats black as coal, white as milk and grey as woodsmoke.

The lightning was gone, and with it the sight of the returning kings. But already the battle had begun to waver, and the whisper went round, 'Carbonel! Carbonel is back! The kings are home again!' And as the fighting gradually faltered and came to a standstill, the shifting mass was jewelled with pairs of glowing eyes, as one by one more and more of the battle-scarred animals turned and looked up to where the kings stood on the bank above them.

'What is this unseemly brawling?' asked Carbonel, and although he did not seem to raise his voice, it cut through the shuffle and murmur of the animals below so that the farthest cat on the Swimming Bath Slopes heard every syllable.

'Is this the way you greet your king? It seems that much has happened since I went away, and there is much for me to learn.'

There was a crash of thunder and another lightning

flash which showed the sea of upturned cat faces below them, and as the thunder rumbled into silence, Rosemary felt a large wet raindrop fall on the hand still holding the matchbox.

'Tomorrow I will hear all about this night's work, and justice shall be done. Until then, home with you where you belong!'

There was a shuffle and a murmur in the darkness below them.

'We go, O Carbonel!' came the answer.

The lamps of a hundred gleaming eyes seemed to go out one by one, as the shamed animals turned away. There was a sighing, rustling noise as they surged past John and Rosemary and streamed away in the darkness. One final lightning flash showed Rosemary a curious sight. A wave of animals reached the edge of what in daylight was the garage roof, and with one movement, like a drift of snow when the thaw sets in, the dark mass slid to the ground, then broke up and disappeared.

The thundery rain was falling in slow heavy drops by now, and the deep blueness of the night began to change to the thin grey that comes before the dawn. Dimly John and Rosemary could see the dark mass of Carbonel and the kings.

A deep voice said, 'We must be on our way, brothers, we have far to travel.'

'This night's work makes us the more anxious to return to see what awaits us.'

Somebody laughed.

'Go on your way, my friends!' said Carbonel. 'And may your homecoming be more peaceable than mine!'

Against the sky, the two children saw them go, a splendid procession of cats of every kind and colour.

One thing they disagreed about afterwards. Rosemary was quite sure that on every head there was a small, shining crown, but John said she imagined it. When they turned back and looked where Carbonel sat alone, he certainly wore no crown. The curves and broken lines of Cat Country seemed to waver and straighten as though they had been redrawn with a ruler. Then they realized they were no longer standing on grass but upon the wet tiles of the garage roof with their elbows on the coping of the roof of Fallowhithe Swimming Baths.

'Father!' called Calidor. 'I pushed a great, grownup tabby right out of Cat Country, honest I did. But I don't like getting my paws wet,' he added plaintively.

The rain was pouring down now. 'Let's go and shelter in the bicycle shed!' said John.

John and Rosemary sat on the rack which in the daytime held the bicycles, and Carbonel perched himself on the saddle of a machine that for some reason someone had forgotten to collect. Calidor strutted around, still full of excitement over his part in the fight, and singing a rather conceited little song. They were joined by Woppit, who had an indignant Pergamond beside her. The old cat had refused to let her join in, and together they had watched from the safety of a distant chimney pot. Merbeck was there too. He had to be supported by Tudge because he was so exhausted.

The rain drummed on the tin roof above them, but nobody noticed it. Carbonel listened in silence to the long story. His golden eyes moved from one to another as they took up the tale in turn. When the threat to Blandamour and the kittens was told, his ears flattened and his tail lashed angrily. But when

Rosemary opened the matchbox on the palm of her hand and the minute white cat stepped delicately out, he did not know whether to growl in fury or purr with pleasure that Blandamour was at least safe. In the end he did neither, and his tiny wife stretched up and licked his nose with a tongue which was no larger than the petal of a scarlet pimpernel, but was none the less loving for that. Carbonel's eyes were troubled. Even Miss Dibdin, whom John had put down on the paving stones beside him, still inside the potted meat jar in case someone should tread on her, seemed to fill the Cat King with grave concern.

'There is much to think about in your story,' said Carbonel. 'Two things only are clear; first that my family and the cats of my kingdom can never pay the debt we owe to John and Rosemary.'

Rosemary blushed a rosy red and John made embarrassed noises in his throat.

'Secondly,' went on Carbonel, 'Mrs Cantrip must be curbed and the magic undone once and for all. But it has been a long night for all of us. Tomorrow we will meet again.'

'In the Green Cave after breakfast?' suggested John. Carbonel nodded.

'And until then I leave my dear Blandamour in your charge.'

'I've thought of the very place!' said Rosemary. 'My old doll's house, and Miss Dibdin can keep her company!'

31

The Final Magic

WHEN John and Rosemary reached home again, the
rain had stopped, and the rising sun gilded the wet
streets and roofs of Cranshaw Road as though they
were made of beaten gold. They were too sleepy to
do anything when they crept indoors except pull Rosemary's old doll's house out from the bottom of her
wardrobe. She had not played with it for years, as was
clear from the jumble of furniture inside. However,
she put the tiny bed on its feet again and made it as
comfortable as she was able with folded handkerchiefs.
Released from the potted meat jar, Miss Dibdin, still
in a dazed condition, climbed gratefully in and Blandamour curled up beside her. The two miniature creatures seemed to find comfort in each other's company.

'It's a funny thing,' yawned John as they latched
the front of the little house, 'but I found it quite difficult to hear Carbonel talking last night. His voice
seemed faint and far away.'

'Just because we're so tired, I expect,' said Rosemary. 'Come on, let's go to bed.'

They slept late that morning, but they woke as re-
freshed as if the night's adventure had been nothing
but a dream.

After breakfast Rosemary tidied up the doll's house.
She gave Blandamour a tiny piece of fish and half a
thimbleful of milk, and from her own breakfast she
saved a piece of bacon the size of a postage stamp for
Miss Dibdin, and a crumb of bread and butter. She

even made her some tea in a doll's house teacup with a single tea leaf.

'Let's take the whole caboodle down to the Green Cave,' said John, so they carried it down between them.

Raindrops still glistened like diamonds on the leaves of the currant bushes. Carbonel was already there, sitting on the biscuit tin, and Merbeck with Tudge, who seemed to have taken on himself the job of personal attendant to the old Councillor. Calidor and Pergamond played about among the fallen leaves, with Woppit sitting at a respectful distance. The leaves of the currant bushes were beginning to change to yellow and orange.

Carbonel studied the doll's house with great interest.

'A palace for my lovely Queen, and conjured up at a moment's notice! That is the sort of little attention I appreciate,' he said.

'Did all the Broomhurst cats go back?' asked John.

'They went,' said Carbonel grimly. 'A rain-soaked, shamefaced collection! There will be no more trouble with them. My old friend Castrum, the husband of Grisana, was so deeply ashamed of his wife's wickedness that he has given up his throne to his son Gracilis. He will make a fine ruler. He is a bachelor, but some day we hope, his father and I, that Pergamond –'

'Your voice is awfully faint, Carbonel,' said John. 'We can hardly hear you speak. What is happening?'

'The power of the red mixture is wearing off. You can take another spoonful, but not until the power of the first has entirely worn off. You had better bring the bottle with you.'

'Bring it with us? Where to?' asked Rosemary.

'Fairfax Market,' said Carbonel. 'We have work to do. First the minuscule magic must be undone. A wife who fits into a matchbox, though in many ways exquisitely beautiful, is a little inconvenient, and I dare say the little human –'

A torrent of tiny twittering came from Miss Dibdin, which they took to mean that she, too, disliked being no larger than a fountain pen.

'Secondly,' went on Carbonel, 'although Mrs Cantrip has no more magic left, she is so set in her wicked ways that she will go on making mischief for someone for the rest of her life unless something is done.'

'Wait a minute while I get Miss Dibdin's travelling jar,' said Rosemary.

There was a further agitated twittering from Miss Dibdin. Rosemary put her head as far as she was able into the doll's house. By standing on the tiny table, the little creature was just tall enough to reach Rosemary's ear, and by shouting as loudly as she could, she managed to make herself understood.

'Not a potted meat jar,' Miss Dibdin said indignantly. 'So undignified!'

Rosemary ran back to the flat and returned with a green glass jar with a bow around the neck that had once contained bath salts. Carrying the jar with Miss Dibdin, and the matchbox with Blandamour curled inside, John and Rosemary headed the procession for Fairfax Market.

'Perhaps it would help if we found something to keep Mrs Cantrip busy,' said Rosemary. 'Then she wouldn't have time for much mischief.'

They had just reached the house as she spoke.

'It looks as though she's been pretty busy already,' said John.

The lace curtains were gone from the window. Over the top, on a board which had been newly nailed, was some wobbly lettering, the paint still wet. It read:

K. CANTRIP, GREENGROCER
By Special Appointment to Her Majesty the Queen.

Displayed below was a box lid full of nettles and another of dandelions, a tray full of clumps of whitish stalks which might have been celery but which Rosemary suspected were hemlock. There were one or two jam jars containing a dark brown substance labelled HENBANE HONEY, and a soup plate full of toadstools of every colour of the rainbow supported a notice which said, 'Try them with bacon.'

'We aren't a minute too soon!' said John. 'Come on!'

The shop door was open as though to welcome early customers. Mrs Cantrip was sitting beside the counter she had arranged, slowly printing something on a piece of cardboard.

'Good morning! What can I do for you?' she said, barely looking up from her work.

'You can give me back my Queen!' said Carbonel.

At the sound of his voice, her pen dug deep into the cardboard in a spatter of ink. Carbonel leapt on to the counter. The black cat and the old woman stared at each other through narrowed eyes.

'So you're back, are you? Why should I give you back your Queen?' said Mrs Cantrip harshly.

'Because your day is over and your power is done!'

The old woman looked around at the ring of accusing faces. Merbeck, Tudge and Woppit had joined Carbonel on the counter. Even the kittens stared with angry eyes from the safety of Rosemary's shoulder.

'You're all against me!' she said at last. 'Just when I've turned honest shopkeeper!'

'Honest!' said John indignantly. 'What about those toadstools? Have you ever tried them with bacon?'

'I shouldn't be so silly,' said Mrs Cantrip scornfully. 'I can't help what my customers do, can I? Well, can I?'

'And the "Special Appointment to Her Majesty the Queen",' said Rosemary. 'That couldn't be true!'

'I never said which queen, did I?' snapped the old woman. 'There's a queen bee I know comes to my garden regular.'

'But you can't go on like this!' said Rosemary. 'Think of all the trouble and anxiety you've caused us. And then there's Queen Blandamour and poor Miss Dibdin. Why, you're crying! I believe you're sorry!'

Two hard, round tears fell from Mrs Cantrip's dimmed eyes, and steered an uneven course down her wrinkled cheeks.

'Sorry?' said Mrs Cantrip. 'Ah, I'm sorry right enough, but not because I made a bit of bother, not me. As promising a bit of mischief as ever I had a hand in. I'm sorry because I didn't enjoy it. And when a witch doesn't enjoy her wickedness any more, it means she's finished, done for!'

'But surely you could enjoy doing something else if you only tried?' asked John.

'Only if I could do the final magic, and I won't ever be able to do that.'

'But why not?'

'Because I can't do it by myself. To make it work, not one, but two people must give up the thing they value most for my sake.'

'But what will the final magic do to you?' asked Rosemary.

'It will turn me into what I might have been if I'd not taken up with the ways of darkness.'

'And if you make this final magic,' said Carbonel, 'what of my Queen, my Blandamour and this . . . this potted person here?' He waved toward Miss Dibdin, who was anxiously peering over the edge of the green glass jar which stood on the counter.

'The spell that changed me would undo all that is left of my magic. They'd become their own size sure enough. But what's the good of talking? Who'd give a bent farthing for me, let alone their dearest possession?'

'I would!' said Rosemary.

'And so would I!' said John stoutly.

'Think well what you're saying,' said Mrs Cantrip.

'I'd give up my new cricket bat!' said John.

'I'd give my sewing box. It's inlaid with mother of pearl, and it belonged to my great-grandmother,' said Rosemary.

'Think well, think well!' said Mrs Cantrip again. For a moment her eyes looked large and appealing as they might have done when she was a girl. The slyness seemed to have been wiped from her face as though with a sponge, leaving nothing behind but a deep anxiety. 'It must be the most precious thing you have, or it's no good!'

'Oh, John,' said Rosemary. 'Do you remember what we said in the wood yesterday – that being able to hear Carbonel and the animals talk was the most exciting thing that had happened to us, and that we couldn't bear it to be taken away?'

John pressed his lips tightly together. He was very pale, but he nodded.

'Oh, Carbonel!' said Rosemary. 'Must it be that?'

'If that is your most precious possession, and if you want to save Mrs Cantrip and undo her magic, it must.'

Very slowly John drew from his pocket the bottle of red mixture.

'Come into the garden,' said Mrs Cantrip, and led the way.

The garden was much the same as the last time Rosemary had seen it, on the day when she had escaped in the flying chair. The curious weeds were still neatly staked, and the beehive stood in the corner.

Mrs Cantrip moved the garden seat from the little square of grass. Then, in the middle of the grass, she spread the scarlet headscarf with the black squiggles. She looked around.

'Seven! I must have seven living things of a kind.'

'We are seven cats!' said Carbonel, and with Merbeck, Tudge and Woppit, the two kittens and Blandamour, they made a ring round the red scarf, nose to tail.

'Can you do it without a book?' asked John.

Mrs Cantrip nodded.

'Every witch carries the final magic in her head. Give me the bottle.'

Very slowly John handed her the red mixture and watched her take her place in the centre of the red-silk, cat-ringed square.

'Good-bye, Tudge, Woppit and Blandamour,' said Rosemary, her eyes hot with tears.

'Good-bye! Good-bye,' said John.

'Not good-bye,' said Carbonel, and his voice was so faint that the two children had to bend down to hear him. 'You may not hear us talk again,' he said, 'but you will always hear us purr. Your fame will stretch far and wide, and cats of Fallowhithe will sing songs about you to their children and their children's children. Whenever any of them purr beneath your stroking fingers, it will be a purr of gratitude, an echo of what my Queen and I will feel always in our hearts. Do not look so sad. Listen, and perhaps we can ease your ...'

The last word was so faint that they could not hear it. They were standing side by side, and in her misery Rosemary clutched John's hand. Mrs Cantrip was standing very stiff and straight. She took the cork from the bottle and poured the red mixture which would have made it possible for them to hear again, not only cats talking, but the birds in the trees, the little scuttling wood creatures, the tiny things that crawl and fly and burrow. She poured it in a ring around the seven cats. They saw her lips move silently as, with her eyes closed, she said the final magic.

Then the purring began. Carbonel began first, loud and clear, not on two pulsing notes as he usually did, but in many notes that made a solemn tune. Then Merbeck joined in, and the two sounds merged and then parted like the instruments of an orchestra. And like the instruments of an orchestra the purrs of Tudge and Woppit joined in, weaving around each other, up and down, now loud, now soft, with Calidor and Pergamond supplying their light treble, making the sweetest music they had ever heard.

John and Rosemary listened, delighted, for how long they did not know, but gradually the sorrow seemed to lift from their hearts, and although their eyes filled with tears, they were not hot tears of unhappiness. Through them the outline of Mrs Cantrip seemed to swell and waver.

'Lend me a hankie,' said John unsteadily. 'I've lost mine.'

They took it in turns to wipe their eyes and noses, and when they looked up again they thought at first that Mrs Cantrip had gone. In her place was a tall, upright old lady. Over her neat cotton dress, she wore a gardening apron, and a pair of leather gardening gloves were on her hands. She looked down at John and Rosemary with eyes that twinkled kindly over her rather large nose.

'You know,' she said as though they were in the middle of a conversation, 'animals can always tell when you like them. That's why so many pussies come to see me.'

She bent down and stroked a magnificent white cat with blue eyes which was sitting at her feet.

'Blandamour!' whispered Rosemary. 'I'm so glad you are your right size again.'

'There is no doubt that you like cats, too!' said Mrs Cantrip.

Blandamour and Carbonel were weaving in and out between the two children, pressing so hard against their bare legs that they found it quite hard to keep their balance. Merbeck, Tudge and Woppit had slipped away. Both children fell on their knees beside the black and the white cat.

'Come and see us sometimes!' whispered Rosemary, and as if in answer a rough tongue licked her cheek.

John stirred Calidor and Pergamond with his foot. They were rolling over each other in an effort to rub themselves against his right ankle.

'Be good kittens!' he said.

With a little 'prrt!' Blandamour called her children to her. One behind the other, Carbonel leading, they trotted away. When they reached the flower bed they paused, gave a quick look back, and disappeared.

'I say!' said John. 'The high wall has gone!' In its place was a low fence which let the sun come streaming in. Instead of hemlock, nettles and deadly nightshade, there were roses, tiger lilies, and round, scarlet dahlias; there were marigolds and nasturtiums and sweet-scented stock.

Mrs Cantrip was cutting a bunch of sweet peas which she said were for Mrs Brown, and while she snipped away she talked over her shoulder.

'Very good of Mr Fudge to give me the morning off. But of course after working with him for so long . . . What's the matter, dear?'

'Hedgem and Fudge? Do you work there?' asked Rosemary.

'Of course! I've been dispensing for him for years.'

John and Rosemary looked at each other in a puzzled way.

'Luckily Albert Flackett is back at work again,' she went on. 'He seems quite recovered, and he tells me he and Myrtle are getting married soon. I'm so glad! Ah, here comes Dorothy with the lemonade.'

They turned. Miss Dibdin, her own size and none the worse for her adventure, was coming out of the house carrying a tray with two glasses on it. She gave no sign of anything except pleasure at their approval of the lemonade. The children drank it politely.

'Miss Dibdin,' said John, as he replaced his empty glass on the tray. 'Have you known Mrs Cantrip for long?'

Miss Dibdin laughed comfortably.

'Why, Katie and I have been friends since we both wore plaits. We were at school together!'

'It's very puzzling,' John said on the way home as they turned to look back at the front of the house. The neat front door was pale yellow now, and golden linen curtains hung at the windows, which were edged with flower-filled window boxes.

'I suppose the magic had to work backwards,' said Rosemary. 'Mrs Cantrip couldn't become what she might have been, without having been all the other things she might have been before.'

John nodded. He seemed to understand, as I hope you do, too.

'How kind of Mrs Cantrip!' said her mother when Rosemary gave her the bunch of sweet peas from Mrs Cantrip's garden.

'Mother, have you known her for long?'

'Why, she's one of my oldest customers!' said Mrs Brown.

'She has lived with that friend of hers – Miss Dibdin – ever since I can remember,' said Mr Featherstone, who was suddenly there again. 'I'm just going down to my apartment for a minute – I've left a large block of ice cream on the kitchen table. Your mother and I thought we ought to have a celebration. Come with me, John.'

John went off with Mr Featherstone. Mrs Brown had buried her face in the bunch of sweet peas.

'I think Mr Featherstone ought to have an elevator put in. Then he wouldn't have to keep running up and down the stairs when he comes to see us every day,' said Rosemary.

Her mother lifted her face from the bunch of flowers. It was as pink as the sweet peas.

'I can think of a better plan, darling,' she said. 'Supposing he came to live here with us. Would you like that, Rosie?' She paused for a moment, and then she said with a rush, 'We're going to be married!'

Rosemary's eyes were round as saucers.

'Mummy, how lovely!' she said.

As she spoke, John came bursting in, and by the way he pumped Mrs Brown's hand up and down and grinned from ear to ear, it was quite clear that he had been let into the secret and entirely approved. As for Mr Featherstone, he said shyly, 'Will I do, Rosie? I'll take such care of you both!'

'I should just think you will do!' said Rosemary, and they laughed and talked until Mrs Brown said, 'My goodness, the chicken will be ruined!' and rushed into the kitchen. But it was not ruined, it was cooked to a turn. When they had all eaten as much as they could manage, Rosemary gave a great sigh.

'A father, and a high school, and chicken for dinner altogether. How perfectly gorgeous!'

The wedding was a quiet one, but among the guests were Mrs Cantrip and Miss Dibdin. As Mr and Mrs Featherstone left the church, not only a black cat, but a snow-white one as well, ran across their path as though to wish them luck.